The Reluctant Heiress

The Reluctant Heiress

JANET TEMPLETON

DOUBLEDAY & COMPANY, INC.
GARDEN CITY, NEW YORK
1987

This Large Print Edition contains the complete, unabridged text of the original Doubleday edition.

All of the characters in this book are fictitious, and any resemblance to actual persons, living or dead, is purely coincidental.

4/87 16.95 Doubleday : City

Library of Congress Cataloging-in-Publication Data

Templeton, Janet, 1926–
The reluctant heiress.

1. Large type books.   I. Title.
[PS3558.E78R4   1987]   813'.54   86-24142
ISBN 0-385-23982-3 (lg. print)
Copyright © 1986 by Morris Hershman
All Rights Reserved
Printed in the United States of America
First Large Print Edition

116693

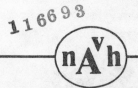

**The Production Review Committee of the
NATIONAL ASSOCIATION
FOR VISUALLY HANDICAPPED
has found this book to meet its criteria
for large type publications.**

To the copy editors at Doubleday who have worked on my books. Your skills have given readers the impression that the novels of Janet Templeton are written by a scholar and grammarian.

Contents

The Reluctant Heiress

CHAPTER 1
Will of Iron

The young lady descended from the family carriage to the city street. Sunlight reflecting from the nearby plane trees appeared to tint her black clothes with green, which enhanced the bright red hair straying from under her poke bonnet and added inestimably to that freshness which nature had generously given her.

"We'll be inside in moments, Aunt," she said.

"I know, dear," the older woman agreed tonelessly as she was helped out of the carriage by the family coachman. She, too, was dressed in unrelieved black, but the sun's presence brightened her demeanor not at all.

Three months had passed since aunt and niece had gone into mourning. The younger had been chafing under that restrictive arrangement for more than eight weeks. It was possible to be grieved and distressed, both, but not to give over all days and nights to such feelings when one was no more than eighteen years of age. Unfortunately, Miss Pamela Forrest had not yet reached the level of understanding at which she could forgive herself for the casual smile or the agreeable thought or the concern for others of the living that often crowded in upon her sensibilities.

"To think that I would see this day," said Aunt Rosemary at Pamela's side. The older woman spoke quietly, as if no tears were left inside her.

Pamela extended an arm to Aunt Rosemary and moderated her own pace as both began the brief walk. Every one of the old houses in this square called Lincoln's Inn Fields was devoted to the offices of solicitors. It was to the nearest that Pamela and her aunt were proceeding in such a stately fashion.

From the corner of an eye Pamela noticed that another carriage, a varicolored brougham, was waiting some ten paces from the Forrest vehicle. Not until she looked directly ahead for the first time did she become aware that a young man's back was clearly to be seen. Its owner was moving briskly to the same house in which Pamela and her aunt were shortly due to appear.

He seemed aware that steps could be heard at his back and accelerated his own pace. At the solid dark door he turned and opened it for the ladies to enter.

His clothes and their fit marked him as a young man of the best class. His top hat was dark, his frock coat the same, his white collar turned down faultlessly over a tie of many colors knotted with care that the late Mr. Brummell would have reluctantly approved, and his tight trousers were of a dark but not mournful hue. In physical appearance he was tall and dark-haired with a slightly redder skin than was usual among men of Pamela's acquaintance.

"Thank you, sir," said Pamela, eyes downcast with the coquetry that was thought by many to pass for maidenly modesty.

She didn't know whether or not to smile when she looked back up after the briefest possible pause. Very likely Aunt Rosemary wouldn't forgive her for showing that much in the way of human feeling at such a time. By nature Pamela may not have been perpetually as merry as the proverbial grig, but she did have the impulse to acknowledge the presence of a handsome young man with intelligent eyes, and especially one who seemed to have responded happily to the sight of her.

There was no time to consider this point of

etiquette as the young man's drawn-out and un-gloved right hand was gesturing them inside.

Pamela accepted the cue and proceeded at her aunt's side. Because her head was held high in pride the raised threshold caused her to lose her footing if only briefly.

She was immediately aware of the young man's hard hand upon hers, assuring that she would remain vertical. So close was he that his breath seemed to brush lightly against her left cheek.

Keeping as calm as she could, Pamela turned to offer her thanks once more. He was courteously retreating, but not before the sight of his confident movements caused her to form the impression of having danced with him at one time. It seemed beyond credibility that she could have done so and forgotten him.

Disturbed and ashamed of herself for the turmoil within her breast, Pamela nodded gratefully after all, but avoided looking at him. She moved ahead. Aunt Rosemary was almost certainly unaware of the mild contretemps, a circumstance for which Pamela was profoundly grateful.

Although she was finding it difficult to gather her faculties, she was aware of having entered a bare but carpeted hallway which led directly to a small but well-lighted room. A wizened man in shiny clothes climbed to his feet at their arrival, easing his pen into a well that had been carved out of the wood for just that purpose. He mustered a smile with some difficulty and waited.

"This is my aunt, Mrs. Forrest," said Pamela as Aunt Rosemary, too, remained silent. At the point of giving her own name, she decided that to do so would only amount to displaying her scattered wits. "My aunt and I have arrived for the reading of her late husband's last will and testament."

The clerk seemed startled by the presence of a female able to speak rationally in this circumstance. Had he known the full extent of Pamela's present feelings her composure would have dumbfounded him. As it was, he looked unsure how to respond.

The young man, entering the anteroom, said quietly, "Let them in, Passy."

"Yes, my lord," the obsequious clerk said immediately.

So the young man was a peer! The news hardly surprised Pamela. There was an air of authority, of surefootedness and confidence about him. Enviously she wondered about the woman who had captured him, not being able to conceive that he could have avoided some eagle-eyed unmarried female and her wiles.

On that note of muffled vexation, she escorted Aunt Rosemary into the next room and saw to it that the bereaved widow was seated comfortably on a visitor chair of good leather.

"Vincent used to love chairs like these," Aunt Rosemary said weakly, and then looked away. She was doing her best to achieve control over her speech, Pamela saw with gratitude. Even after three months it was difficult for the widow. No clearer explanation could have been offered for her refusal to venture out during the time between Uncle Vincent's death and this afternoon. Any reading of the will before she was prepared to accept the necessary ritual would have resulted in a storm of tears.

"I must tell you," Aunt Rosemary had said during one of the hours when she was poising herself for this first assault upon the outside world as a widow, "that your uncle has provided for you in his will, although I am not aware of any conditions that might be attached to what I am certain must be a typically generous action on my late husband's part. Be certain that you will remain financially secure."

Pamela had insisted truthfully that it wasn't a matter to which she had ever given the least thought.

There was a moment for her to look around this room in which her future was to be discussed with that of others. Along with an unused grate and coal scuttle and yellow velvet curtains that would soon need to be taken down by the staff, there was a mahogany desk that looked as if it had been built into the house. A smell of leather emanated from the bound volumes of legal import that crowded shelves on all four sides of the room.

Aunt Rosemary, aware of the odors and their cause, suddenly quirked her lips at the corners in the beginnings of the first smile that Pamela could recall seeing there for a long time.

"Vincent used to say that lawyers study every phase of their work except the postponing of cases," she said. "Each lawyer is born with a capacity to postpone cases. That is what your uncle often said, too."

She then shuddered, but drew a deep breath in an attempt to continue presenting a dignified exterior. For once she didn't publicly blame herself for being distracted while Uncle Vincent remained buried in St. Faith's Chapel at the east end of the crypt in St. Paul's on Ludgate Hill. Aunt Rosemary was becoming aware of the needs of others with whom she made contact. It was an encouraging sign.

Another person entered the room within the next moments. Pamela, turning, was astonished to see the same youthful and confident-looking peer who had made so firm an impression on her in the street as well as in the anteroom.

"May I ask why you are here?"

The assurance that was so great a part of him remained in spite of his shrug.

"For the life of me I don't entirely know."

"Please clarify that as much as you can."

"I am only able to tell you that I had a written request from Mr. Holt to be here on this day and at this time."

Facing a choice of two conundrums to be resolved, Pamela chose the simplest.

"And may I ask who you are?"

The peer's confidence remained unshaken, but his attitude conveyed that no other person of wealth in the City could possibly lay claim to such a lack of knowledge.

A newcomer coughed.

Whirling around, Pamela confronted the fourth entrant into Mr. Holt's chambers. This was Avery Holt, the son of Uncle Vincent's solicitor and one who was following in his father's vocational path. He was very nearly six feet tall, a disconcerting height that had kept most girls away from him against their wishes and, in many cases, his own. Without this singular affliction, he would have been considered a handsome young man even if clean-shaven. The latter quality was unusual for a servant of Her Majesty's legal system.

"Ma'am, please permit me to express my deep regrets on your bereavement," he said, drawing himself up as if he was even now sitting in the High Court of Probate on the Queen's Bench. "Pamela, my sympathies on the loss of a valued elder. Lloyd, I am happy that you could be here with us."

"Thank you," said the mysterious Lloyd.

Both Pamela and her aunt were too startled by Avery's presence to make any acknowledgment.

Seeing him approach the desk chair, however, Aunt Rosemary stiffened and spoke.

"But where is Cecil?"

"I am sorry to say that my father is ill,

ma'am," said Avery. "He has requested that I do what is necessary on this sad occasion."

Aunt Rosemary subsided, once again causing Pamela to feel better about the older woman's burgeoning recuperative powers.

Politely, as Aunt Rosemary was not wholly ready to be socially adept once again, Pamela said, "I hope that your father isn't indisposed with a serious malady."

"It is continual sneezing that has laid him low, Pamela. You can be sure that such a difficulty is so undignified as not to be worthy of the highest standards of his calling and mine."

Pamela nodded. She had known Avery casually since childhood and even after Pamela's own parents passed away in '29 of the influenza and she came to live with Uncle and Aunt. Avery had communicated occasionally in the years when he served his articles, passed his examinations, and settled into a practice alongside his father.

Never renowned for patience in the teeth of unreasonable delay, Pamela said, "Can we now proceed to the ritual we are here to perform?"

"*Brava!*" the ineffable Lloyd approved softly. Pamela was tempted to turn and smile in response but felt once again that the occasion was inappropriate.

"Of course," Avery agreed a little huffily. As the compere of the afternoon's function, he probably thought that he should set the pace at which events would occur. Nonetheless, he reached into a breast pocket for a case with spectacles. These he affixed to the end of his nose. Whether he required them or not, he must have known that they gave him the look of a Q.C. in full-bottomed wig and stuff robe who was about to ask questions of a recalcitrant witness. "Let us begin."

The first section of the document covered ground that might have been thought of as controversial. Uncle Vincent affirmed that he was of sound and disposing mind, at least half of which must have been correct. Eminently sane though he certainly had been, he was no proper witness to insist on the point.

Bequests of money were made to servants who were not among those present. Aunt Rosemary hadn't wanted witnesses for this occasion, taking the sensible premise that she might otherwise lack control of her feelings in public. Pamela had done her aunt's bidding in this matter. Instructions had been communicated to

Mr. Holt the elder, but these made the presence of Lloyd whoever-he-was all the more difficult to understand.

Although the widow kept a firm halter on her tear ducts, she gave free rein to her tongue. Praise of Vincent's generosity was spoken as soon as an amount was named.

" 'My best violin, the "Joseph" Guarnerius, I give and bequeath to my longtime friend and fellow lover of music, Sir Humphrey Packwood.' "

"I am so glad that Humphrey will be getting the violin," Aunt Rosemary said, leaning over to whisper in her niece's ear. "Playing together was a happiness that they often shared."

Pamela nodded sadly, recollecting a certain winter's day when it first became clear to her that Uncle Vincent had earned more money in business than he and Aunt Rosemary would ever need. She had asked why he didn't pursue his deepest remaining interest from then on and become a respected artist in the concert halls.

" 'Pon my word, I don't know," he had responded, hiding his discomfort in a massive shrug. "Possibly I begrudge myself so much happiness."

Never before had Pamela felt sorry for someone older than her eighteen years and a member of the other sex as well. The memory caused her to bow her head. A wealthy man's life had concluded without its owner experiencing his idea of the ultimate gratification which it could have been possible for him to know, a life concluded without having been lived to the fullest.

" 'My remaining property and moneys,' " Avery resumed, adjusting the spectacles once again and raising the foolscap sheets because they were probably so far from him that a man of his height couldn't see them too readily.

It developed that the "said" property and moneys, as Uncle Vincent referred to them after the first mention, were bequeathed to his dear wife. Aunt Rosemary's control of herself was barely proof against this onslaught of feeling. She breathed heavily. Pamela plied her with a cambric square in case of need. Aunt Rosemary eventually sniffed and resigned herself to a strained silence, over which it was possible to discern the injunction from Uncle Vincent that she should permit matters to be handled by the trusted firm of Holt and Holt.

Pamela could hardly help glancing to one side. Lloyd whoever-he-was sat with head lowered. It did seem extraordinary that no time had yet been given to a consideration of whatever matter had caused him to be asked to attend this proceeding. Surely he, like herself, was the object of some important bequest.

Sensing that he was under examination, the peer raised his head. Those probing gray eyes caught hers. It was Pamela who looked away hurriedly in the knowledge that she was blushing to the tips of her ears. The frivolous thought had crossed her mind that he knew the steps of every currently popular dance and could even go the wrong way on the ball floor when he wished to do so. Very likely he knew much about females as well. It was this latter thought which had primarily caused the blush that was shaming her on this of all possible occasions.

Avery continued at his duty, reaching a sentence in which it was made clear that Aunt Rosemary would provide at her discretion for the future welfare of Pamela's twelve-year-old brother, Ian, who also lived with them. Ian had very properly been excused from making an appearance at this saddening time.

Avery suddenly lowered the spectacles on his nose and peered over them at the auditors. "I wish to state that the final bequest in its complete form is highly unusual. My father is certainly aware of it. Looking at the document for the first time, I, too, am cognizant of this."

Pamela, having offered yet a second cambric square to her aunt, noticed from the corner of an eye that Avery's stare rested on her. It seemed as if he was expecting difficulties over the next minutes and felt that the obstacles would come from her.

" 'I direct,' " Avery proceeded with his recitation, " 'that the sum of twenty-five thousand pounds be sequestered for use as a dowry to be given upon the marriage of my niece, Pamela Forrest, the daughter of my late brother.' "

Pamela was so stunned that she didn't notice the solicitor's voice rising on the last word, as if more remained to be said. Unable to respond directly at this proof of her late uncle's generosity, she looked down and closed her eyes tightly.

Aunt Rosemary blew her nose as an indication that she, too, had been moved. "Dear Vincent always cared about you and Ian as he would have cared for children of his and mine."

Pamela nodded. Feelings of numbness pervaded her body from the neck down, or so it seemed.

Avery cleared his throat and continued upon the course that Uncle Vincent had set for him.

" 'I am not sure that my dear niece, although serious by nature, would be prudent enough to choose a mate who can bestow upon her the social position that would be best for herself and any children of hers.' "

It was as if her uncle was offering a final lecture after the many that he had given directly. More than once he had said that she ought not to test young men by discussing with them a number of the inequities that displeased her in society, particularly the casual treatment of women. Uncle Vincent did love her, but he wanted her to be more like one of those females with no outlet for their energies except that of capturing a husband when single and then devoting their married lives to one unimportant matter after another.

" 'This sum is to be given,' " Avery was reading, the foolscap held at arm's length as if he expected it to jump up at him otherwise, " 'on the day that my niece marries the son of my departed but consenting friend, Rupert Wilcoxen. I refer to Lloyd Wilcoxen, the fourth Earl of Kinnon.' "

And as the cannon shell struck, Avery put down the foolscap on his desk. Plainly he was glad to have given up all contact with it.

CHAPTER 2
Prophet and Loss

Upon hearing the name, Pamela's outrage at the condition of this bequest was almost relegated to the back of her mind. Vividly she now recollected dancing the *valse* with Lloyd Wilcoxen, not then a peer, at a ball given by Miriam Packwood's parents. A splendid dancer he had indeed proved himself, as well as an almost frighteningly handsome man, but there was a difficulty in pursuing a friendship that might deepen into something finer.

Lloyd Wilcoxen was known as one of the devil-may-cares of society, a Fashionable who gambled heavily and pursued women with an energy that should have been spent on worthier objectives. A man who cared nothing for responsibilities, obviously, for improving the lot of others or even pursuing a career at some enterprise. Small wonder that one violet-eyed beauty, at least, hadn't evinced the slightest interest in him when he seemed willing to acquaint himself with her!

And now it was apparent that Uncle Vincent and Lloyd's father had got together and decided wickedly to resolve the marital quest that the two might be making separately. If the son and daughter of old friends were to marry, it would be a final opportunity to dominate the futures of others from Beyond. No doubt it had been a reasonable assumption that neither Pamela nor Lloyd would become seriously interested in others before both older men were carried off to their rewards.

It was almost impossible for Pamela to feel anger toward that relative who had done so much for her and her young brother as well. Sadness pervaded her first response. Uncle Vincent, of all men, had known the agony of not having the life he wanted. His ambition to be a violinist on the concert stage had been unsettled by the demands of business and then by the feeling, as he had partly explained, of being more accustomed to the dull ache of frustration in that area than to the notion of happiness.

And it was this man, this beloved relative, who had sentenced her to matrimony with a feckless stranger!

She was expected to say something. Aunt Rosemary had turned with a tentative smile. Avery, having restored his reading spectacles to the steel case intended for them, was looking as if prepared to rise to his full height and attempt to intimidate her if necessary.

The Earl's response wasn't plain, as he happened to have ensconced himself back of her. Nevertheless she did hear Kinnon, as she would probably think of him from now on, get to his feet.

"I had no idea what was planned," he said as the others' eyes moved in his direction. "My guv'nor wasn't above supporting whatever schemes he felt would be best for me to follow."

"And my uncle as well," Pamela said at last. Her voice sounded rusty.

Aunt Rosemary, buoyed by the fact that Pamela hadn't burst into tears at this settling of her future, spoke calmly.

"What a dear generous man my Vincent was," she said, correctly on the whole, and not for the first time. "What a lovely bride you will be!"

Pamela's consent was now taken for granted. It would have been impossible to make any statement about the full extent of her feelings.

Kinnon, under no such restrictions except for the courtesies imposed by the presence of the widow, astonished Pamela by prefacing his next remark with a friendly chuckle.

"Certainly I am deeply honored by Mr. Vincent Forrest's confidence in me as a suitable husband for Miss Pamela." He smiled, adding a friendly inclination of the head. "I feel certain that she and I are going to give this vital matter our most sympathetic consideration."

Pamela found herself incensed at Kinnon for seeming amused at the fiat handed down by one old man with the consent of another. He would have won Pamela's admiration by indicating the desire to make a protest that might shatter the rafters of this book-lined cell of Avery's and Mr. Holt's.

Quietly, because of the regard she felt for her aunt, Pamela said, "Sympathetic consideration has already been given to this matter, my lord, by your late father and my late uncle."

Her tone must have been more revealing of pent-up anger than she had expected. Every eye in the room had returned to her.

"I wish to cast no aspersions upon you, my lord, but I will not submit under any circumstances to this order."

Aunt Rosemary appeared to recoil without moving. "Do you mean that you would betray the wishes of the dearest man who ever lived?"

"My disobedience cannot affect him any longer," Pamela pointed out.

She was too angry at the Earl to understand that he was attempting to soothe troubled waters.

"Perhaps, Miss Pamela, we can meet for a discussion of the matter."

"Thank you, but I do not see that there would be any use in our doing so." She was regretful only because the company of a handsome man was always pleasurable in itself, but undeniable limits had become apparent in the current difficulty. "I cannot submit to blackmail from beyond the grave."

She caught the sudden appreciative glint in his eyes but was unable to examine his reaction in further detail. Aunt Rosemary had drawn a deep breath.

One careful look showed that the older woman was not, however, in tears. Pamela was grateful, although she no longer felt that a small miracle had taken place. The last minutes had made it clear that Aunt Rosemary was willing to cry for her dead, but not over the quirks of those who remained alive.

"Perhaps we should leave now, Aunt."

"Yes, I agree," said Pamela's remarkable relative.

Avery's long legs returned him in the briefest possible time from the adieux made before the carriage of aunt and niece, to which he had courteously escorted them. In the discussion area, as he had taken to calling that room in which clients were received, he found his long-time friend, the Earl, looking out the curtained window. The canoe landau in which the ladies rode was proceeding at the stateliest of paces.

Kinnon, to call him by Pamela's identification, turned as the carriage left his sight.

"Fascinating," he said before turning once again to his friend. "Entirely fascinating."

Avery understood that it wasn't himself or the aunt who had drawn Kinnon's encomiums.

"I have known Pamela for many years," he responded, and then gave the massive shrug by which he usually indicated that a girl was too lacking in height for him to consider her as anything but an acquaintance.

"My recollection is of dancing with her at Sir

Humphrey Packwood's," Kinnon said. "It happened a while before my guv'nor passed away. Miss Forrest seemed to dismiss me as being a rakehell."

"As indeed you have been," said his friend.

Kinnon's mind remained on the subject of Miss Pamela Forrest. She was a young lady of decided prejudices and opinions, nor did she have the least hesitation about ventilating these. Such a course of action wasn't invariably wise, as Kinnon himself had good reason to know.

His own venturing to express a controversial point of view had resulted in the greatest difficulty of his relatively young life. In a debate at Oxford he had been instructed to argue the position that Britain must give up her colonial possessions, a concept about which he had never held strong opinions and one which seemed almost certain to prove unpopular at Brasenose itself.

He had taken care to speak well and pointedly. In a hall filled with students whose degrees as Bachelors of Civil Law would likely impel them toward a career in governmental administration, Lloyd Wilcoxen's persuasive advocacy had resulted in his being adjudged the victor at this debate. The Chancellor promptly and

mechanically praised himself for allowing various points of view to be heard in debate. His
praises had been immediately echoed by the
Vice-Chancellor, the group of Pro-Vice-Chan-
cellors, the High Steward, the Proctors, and the
Pro-Proctors. Otherwise, these gentry had been
quite cool toward him. Two days after the start
of the Trinity term Lloyd had been sent down
on an excuse without the least foundation in
fact. He formed the impression of being sneered
at from the moment he left Brasenose itself and
all along the curve of Oxford's High Street,
from Magdalen to St. Martin's.

The guv'nor had taken this matter very badly,
refusing to believe that any defense could be
offered on his son's behalf. Seriously he had suggested sending the boy to that small town in
Perthshire from which his family title had been
taken, a town the guv'nor himself had early left
for the City and wouldn't return to except for
some urgent but blessedly rare ceremonial occasion. Lloyd had made it a point to agree about
being cast into outer darkness but deftly post-
poned the actual event. His future was still in
the process of negotiation when the guv'nor
passed away and he inherited the title. The episode and its aftermath had effectively taught

him a lesson about the evils of disputatiousness and the beneficent effects of appearing cooperative in trying circumstances. It was a tenet he had demonstrated briefly in dealing with the distressing situation which had just developed.

"I can foresee difficult times ahead for Miss Forrest," Kinnon said.

"Certainly, if she makes a point of being overtly contrary." Avery nodded. "She will be accused of disrespect to an elder and of not regarding the wish of that person who did so much for her."

"What is to be done in order to aid this girl?" Kinnon asked. There was a pause, occasioned by Avery's inability to conceive of a stratagem. "Could I make it clear that we disagree about marriage?"

"You'll be tarred with the same brush if you do." Avery could offer criticism for any idea that might be mentioned, it seemed. "Your father consented to this course of action."

"I might take flight for, let us say, one of the American states."

"You won't do that," Avery remarked, unerringly putting a finger on the major drawback to that scheme.

It was true. Kinnon sat in the Lords these

days and worked effectively behind the scenes to smooth the process in the reading out of certain bills whose contents he approved in whole or in part. His actions had remained a public secret and weren't generally known to such malcontents as Miss Forrest.

"Then we reach no conclusion in this matter," Kinnon said in the flattest tone he could summon.

"I fear not," Avery conceded, sounding almost grateful that nothing had occurred to him that might have stirred the imagination.

Kinnon immediately adopted the one apparent course that didn't involve leaving matters intact.

"I will attempt to speak with the girl," he said, "and persuade her about the advantages of at least pretending to accept the situation."

It had occurred to him before this talk even began that the opportunity for further converse with the violet-eyed young woman would be very welcome to him, very welcome indeed.

"It is over," Pamela said gratefully as she settled back into the canoe landau for the ride home.

Aunt Rosemary responded after a moment's thought. "Another difficulty has now begun."

Her aunt had insisted on keeping the head of the carriage turned up, making it more difficult for Pamela to appreciate the attractions of London on a sunny May afternoon. The strong sun illuminated Nell Gwyn's former residence as the ladies passed, an edifice from which society matrons turned in disgust and which unmarried girls often examined during a flurry of mixed emotions.

Pamela's inspection was interrupted by a comment from her relative.

"A fine-looking man, the Earl is," Aunt Rosemary mused aloud.

"He is a heedless libertine who cares for nothing but his own pleasure."

"Time has been known to reform a rake."

Pamela ventured on a pleasantry. "I don't think that there is any use for a toothless rake."

Aunt Rosemary subsided until the carriage left this hive of legal establishments. Upon passing the Staple Inn at Holborn, she ventured upon another observation.

"The word of your response to your uncle's will is going to be known through the city in a very little while," she said reasonably. "Mr. Holt the elder will certainly make it known. He is capable of retailing a juicy morsel of gossip through hundreds of sneezing fits if he can do it no other way. I am fond of Cecil, as it happens, but truth must be served."

"I can't help what Mr. Holt may do."

A striking change had come over Aunt Rosemary, a change that was plain to her niece. More than once over the last months the older woman had promised that as soon as she could bring herself to arrange a reading of dear Vincent's will she would accept her widowhood and proceed with life as best she could. This she was now doing, not referring to her own grief but attempting to deal with others in her usual reasonable and intelligent manner. Someone who took into account this strong resolve could have safely concluded that Aunt Rosemary was an extraordinary woman.

"Of course you can, child! You have only to agree in public that the marriage will take place."

"But then—"

"Listen to me, please! You agree and later on you break off the engagement. Tell everyone that there was some dispute between the two of you, perhaps that he wanted your favors before the ceremony and you staunchly declined to grant them without the forms of propriety having been observed. The Earl's reputation being what it is, such a statement will be readily believed."

"I cannot do what you say, sensible though it sounds," Pamela said quietly.

"Can you not understand that society will have forgotten the matter in a short time? New sensations will come along. You must appreciate that."

"I will not appear as someone agreeable to the bidding of another who orders me to make a decision that must perforce affect the balance of my life."

"Need I point out that if you follow my counsel, Pamela, you won't be marrying anyone?"

"All of society would be convinced that as a female I am therefore a chattel," Pamela said.

She hadn't wanted to put the matter so unmistakably, dreading a return to unsettled behavior from the older woman. She had once again underestimated Aunt Rosemary, however.

"I do understand that," her aunt said, calmly stroking her chin with delicate fingers. "Was I any less of a chattel when I married Vincent? I was not. Pamela, let me assure you that my father ordered me to marry this gentleman who had a fine future ahead in the world of business. All my creature comforts would be attended to. My parents would be provided for in their old age. My five brothers, who took after my father by being convinced that they would earn money yet had the almost total inability to do so, would be put into sinecures in one of Vincent's enterprises and be secure. I had to be grateful, as my own dear mother told me more than once, that I had attracted the attention of so promising a man."

Pamela refrained from pointing out that the externals of that situation in no way resembled her own.

"I bade a tearful good-bye to Binky Bascomb, whom I had desperately wanted to offer for me and whom I dearly loved. I did my filial duty, Pamela, and found a man who made me exquisitely happy from the marriage day onward. True, we never had children of our own, but surrogates did arrive in time." She raised a palm to halt the burgeoning protest. "What I am saying is that you cannot know beforehand how a marriage will evolve, whether it was contracted for love or money or (as in my case) for duty.

The principle of virtually dictating a marriage, you see, isn't bad in and of itself."

Pamela, who was surprised at hearing the full story of Aunt Rosemary's marriage since only snippets and hints had been vouchsafed to her when younger, nevertheless drew herself up firmly.

"I will not accept that," she said.

They reached New Burlington Street in silence that was baffled on both sides rather than angry. The carriage eased its way over to Clifford Street and the red brick four-story house in which Pamela and her young brother had lived for almost as long as she could remember.

Silently aunt and niece passed the railing that separated this house from the balance of civilization. Aunt Rosemary led the way to the pair of steps before the front door, her reflection caught by the letter-box slit and the brass plate that would have to be replaced by one that displayed her own name. Her body, instead of being softened by her own sadness of these last three months, was made rigid with regret for another human being.

"You won't accept the conditions of the society in which we all live, child," she said, utilizing the form of address that she only made hers in the course of disagreements. "A hard life is ahead of you. Probably you will see that truth fully demonstrated no later than this very night!"

CHAPTER 3
Discord with Music

Pamela soon discovered that her brother had left the house with his tutor, no doubt to learn something of nature in its own habitat. Mr. Gernald, who was Ian's preceptor, believed in empiricism as the sole method of teaching that contained the slightest validity. Presumably Ian knew nothing of wars or the achievements of past statesmen, but it seemed a small price to pay if the boy wasn't exposed to fables about animals who spoke in homilies and children who apparently even prayed in their sleep.

Supper was a wholesome meal beginning with a splendid mock·turtle soup and followed by cutlets with sea kale. The most notable feature was the addition of a cheese *soufflé à la vanille* with the strong tea, the first time a dessert had been offered at table since Uncle Vincent became so terribly ill. Pamela's twelve-year-old brother was rendered comparatively silent by the cornucopia of viands, confining himself to a question about what animal had been murdered in order to produce the dessert. Ian showed signs of becoming a cantankerous grown-up.

The supper was followed by a half hour's ease in the second-floor sitting room. Aunt Rosemary made no further reference to the afternoon's discussion as part of her effort to seem unmoved by emotion. She had dressed in dark blue, which didn't happen to suit her excellently well, in Pamela's view, but seemed startlingly decadent in light of the deep mourning clothes that had sheltered her body over these last months.

Promptly at eight o'clock, Pamela excused herself and walked upstairs to her room. This was small and brightly furnished, with a bed, three comfortable mogadore chairs, a closed-down desk, two round tables with various framed cut-outs from magazines, and book-shelves in which the few improving volumes were placed erect with the title-bearing spines clearly visible, while novels lay flat but in profusion.

The dress that Pamela was to wear on this special night was soon brought in by the upper housemaid. Pamela had been promised the opportunity to attend a small dance at the Boyce residence on the night after Uncle Vincent's will had been read, the first night's pleasure since her uncle's death. Sir Humphrey and Lady Packwood had previously agreed to act as her chaperones for the evening and would soon be calling for her. It behooved Pamela to dress as quickly as was feasible.

The nile-green gown had the effect of softening her bright red hair and illuminating the violet eyes. By some alchemy it also minimized that roundness of her face which was certainly attractive but with certain dresses gave the impression of being nearly bereft of bones. The Saxony cloth lay beautifully across her in its needlework of flowers and vines along with an arabesque border. It did seem, though, as if the cross-laced left sleeve had shrunk in the last months of disuse. That impression however, lasted only a very short time. The upper housemaid, Charity by name, deftly applied herself with a needle and thread, eliminating the difficulty in moments.

Pamela was rigorously inspecting herself in the three-panel mirror when there was a soft knock at her door. It opened on Aunt Rosemary.

"There is unfortunate news," she said, raising a sheet of foolscap in her left hand. "This was just delivered by one of the Packwood house staff."

"Something is wrong, then?"

"Dorothea Packwood is indisposed and Sir Humphrey is loyally staying home with her." Aunt Rosemary sniffed. "I don't doubt that Humphrey is taking advantage of some minor illness to rush into his study and lacerate his violin even further. I dread to think what dear Vincent's beloved Guarnerius will sound like after a few months of Humphrey Packwood's tender mercies."

Pamela's face fell. "Could anyone else act as an escort, to your satisfaction?"

"Many people could, but the hour precludes making the request in time for it to be carried out." Aunt Rosemary looked down at her innate dark blue. "I don't think that my presence in this particular finery will wholly disgrace the Forrest name."

"Oh, Aunt, would you do this for me in spite of our—our recent disagreements?"

"You are still my niece, and a young person must continue to live as happily as may be." Aunt Rosemary's smile became almost as bright as it used to be when she was a married woman. "In twenty minutes I will meet you downstairs."

Not for the first time it occurred to Pamela that her existence was indeed a fortunate one, unlike that of many orphaned females or even those with living parents. It was a point which someone like the Earl of Kinnon would never have appreciated in all its complexity, she felt sure.

The impulse came upon her to embrace the older woman, as she had done before over the years. A moment's consideration, however, persuaded her that Aunt Rosemary might well dissolve into tears at such a show of affection. It was better for the older woman's sake at this time for Pamela to accept the kindness as her due.

"Thank you, dear Aunt," Pamela said quietly and looked away. Her own eyes were swimming in tears.

No sign of moisture remained as the family landau took aunt and niece the short distance to Savile Street and the home of the Marquess and Marchioness of Criddon, along with that of their daughter, Lady Suzanne Boyce. So close a friend of Pamela's was Lady Suzanne that the former always thought of the domestic unit as the Boyces.

She disembarked on the curb, her aunt following. Charity, the upper housemaid, had been conscripted to serve as aide-de-camp should either of the ladies experience sudden difficulty with costuming or coiffure. She waited silently within, prepared to enter the house by the servants' route after the ladies were inside.

Pamela walked to the door and passed the invitations to the third footman, who accepted them with a respectful nod and turned to the stair landing and the second footman's roost.

"Mrs. Forrup and Miss Forrup," he called.

Pamela and her aunt exchanged small smiles, as usual when the family name was mangled by servants during some occasion such as this. Walking up the carpeted landing, Pamela was fully aware of the scents which blanketed this outer area. Every window was three quarters closed against the night air, that harbinger of evil, and the various fragrances seemed almost like physical presences.

The second footman referred to them as Mrs. and Miss Foreman.

"Better," said Pamela under her breath as she and Aunt Rosemary proceeded up to the next level and the drawing room from which sounds of revelry were emanating.

The family butler, who ought to have known Pamela at least, offered his own deferential smile and called out the family name as Forrup, just as the first footman had done. Pamela, who was no longer surprised by any occurrence along these lines, sailed inside to wait behind Aunt Rosemary in greeting their hostess.

She was aware of stronger scents here, and of a babble of conversation among the nervous young and especially those ladies who had to pretend that they were fully occupied although not a male had requested their company in the dance that was now proceeding. A piano and violin duo could be heard busily at a polka. It must have crossed Aunt Rosemary's mind that there was scant justice in the continued existence of a violinist who handled his bow as if it were an ax to chop down a series of trees.

The other sound of which Pamela was suddenly aware was that of one sneeze followed by its duplicate. Recollecting the story that Avery's father, Cecil Holt, was similarly afflicted during this day, she looked around a little anxiously. The gossipy solicitor, a medium-sized man in comparison to his son's excessive height, was indeed on the premises and conversing with a pair she didn't recognize. It was an unfortunate augury, to Pamela's mind. No doubt the news was current about what course had been chosen by one independent-minded young woman defying the instructions of a deceased relative who had done so much to be of assistance to her.

Lady Criddon approached Aunt Rosemary and embraced her and said more than once that it was a privilege to see her. Aunt Rosemary, as her niece could have foretold, was hard put to it to keep from dissolving in tears. The night would be more difficult for her than Pamela could have foreseen, although Aunt Rosemary was likely to have insisted on accompanying her in any case.

To Pamela's shock, Lady Criddon only murmured her name once and offered a small frosty smile. It did seem as if Avery's father had been busily gossiping as well as sneezing.

She passed quickly by, making it a point not to meet Aunt Rosemary's sympathetic glance. The Marquess was speaking delightedly to one of the more attractive guests. No young man requested Pamela to join him in a dance, as nearly always happened after the ritual greeting from a hostess.

Pamela sensed the need for friends at a time like this. Lady Suzanne Boyce was vivaciously speaking with a young man who moved away, most likely at a word from her. She was dressed in royal blue tarletane, which well became her. The relative absence of fripperies about her gown would have earned an approving nod from the young Queen Victoria, as would the sight of blond hair parted in the center and held in place by a tortoiseshell comb. Instead of delightedly approaching her, which Pamela would have expected a younger hostess, so to speak, to do, Lady Suzanne was content for once to await Pamela's arrival and then come forward only for the last two steps.

Despite noises on all sides, the young ladies took time to compliment each other fulsomely on their respective rig-outs. With that much accomplished, Lady Suzanne suddenly looked about to make sure that no one was in earshot and lowered her voice.

"Mr. Cecil Holt is telling everyone that you have refused an inheritance." Clearly the offense rankled with Pamela's friend, and its perpetrator was someone whose very sanity must be suspect.

"I stood up for myself." There could be no need to remind Suzanne once more how alert Pamela had always been to any example of females being treated like chattels, like minor pieces on a chess board. No doubt Pamela's own largely fortunate circumstances had made her more keenly aware of inequities done to others, but that, too, was a point she could forbear repeating. "You do understand, don't you?"

"Oh, certainly, certainly," Lady Suzanne said so quickly that she might not have been listening to every word. "As I hear of these matters, you are being disrespectful to an elder by declining to follow your late uncle's solemn injunction and marry the Earl of Kinnon."

"I object to the order that I must marry a given man," Pamela said, confining herself to a point to which she felt that a friend of hers must certainly respond. "Wouldn't any female with a sense of her own worth feel the same?"

"Anyone with your interests at heart," said Lady Suzanne rather coolly, "would strongly suggest that you not antagonize all of society by being intractable."

"I have refused to do something under duress," Pamela insisted.

"Your choice is made, then. Please excuse me."

Almost unbelievingly, Pamela watched her friend, perhaps her former friend, move across the highly polished floor to greet a newcomer.

One glance at this male arrival's pitch-black

hair and the skin somewhat more sun-touched than that of most fashionable London residents caused her to gasp. This devil-may-care peer had manifested himself at the worst possible time and place, from her point of view. She was sighted quickly by the probing gray eyes. Only another moment passed before the Earl of Kinnon began moving purposefully across the floor in Pamela's direction.

A few seconds must have remained before the calamity, as she found herself ungenerously thinking of Kinnon, was visited upon her. During that brief span, it could be possible to obtain a reprieve.

In this she was optimistic. The way to the nearest set of stairs, adorned by young women who hadn't been asked to dance and were therefore in a modified purgatory, was blocked by the oncoming apparition of the Earl of Kinnon. There was a balcony, but the weather was slightly unseasonable and it would be possible for the alert Kinnon to discover her whereabouts. If she wanted further to avoid him she would have no recourse but to jump. This she was understandably reluctant to do.

The next likely avenue of escape consisted of

finding a partner to move instantly to the dance floor with her.

Avery Holt, Esquire, was on the premises, but he remained wary, as ever, about dancing with females over whom he would certainly tower.

Cecil Holt, Avery's father, with whom she was slightly acquainted, could be seen and heard cheerily talking and sneezing in a corner of the room that wouldn't be accessible if she wanted to avoid any dealings with the infernal Kinnon.

A young man unknown to her was walking about with a languid air that was probably feigned, considering his likely age. Would it be possible to engage his attention?

She smiled, as a way of encouraging him to advance. It seemed ill advised. The young man rubbed a hand over part of his forehead as if to hide the accretion of pimples. He suddenly took a step backward and then another, as if to avoid contamination from an attractive young woman. Two more steps, and then he turned on a heel. Swiftly he resumed his wanderings. Not for the first time Pamela wondered why youthful males paced a ballroom in search of prospective partners when females of all ages and states of comeliness waited within the shortest of possible distances. It did seem as if his search was unlikely to be gratified within the Criddon precincts.

"I don't understand that," said his lordship, the Earl of Kinnon, having reached her at last and commencing a conversation in the middle. "The company of a comely woman is beyond price."

Not recognizing the words as an indirect quotation from one of the effusions of King Solomon, Pamela bridled. Although he had said nothing offensive, indeed he had offered a gratifying look at her in the nile green, she was prepared to be offended. A moment passed before she soothed herself into an appearance of placidity.

His lordship, as was only to be expected, looked well. He wore a frock coat as if it had materialized upon his body one day and would never need removal. With the collar fashionably turned down over the circle of a loosely knotted tie, a frilled shirt front and black trousers, he gave the appearance of a man who didn't concern himself with appropriate garb but was always turned out to perfection.

"Perhaps that young man felt he would be directed to marry me and showed some independence," she snapped.

"Or perhaps he felt that he wouldn't," Kinnon said agreeably.

She reminded herself that she was aggrieved and indignant.

"Can you be cozened onto the dance floor?" his lordship asked with the proper combination of diffidence and certainty of a positive answer.

"Not by you, my lord." She was careful to smile.

"A hit!" said his lordship, drawing a hand to the region of his heart as if wounded. "A palpable hit!"

His serene humor gave the greatest possible impetus to her own irritability. More than anything else, now that he was in close and public proximity, she wanted Kinnon to become angry, too. If they were seen having words, it would be clear to the densest of creatures that these two were ill matched. This small dance, attended by a splendid selection of Fashionables, offered a perfect setting for the minor drama.

"Have you come here tonight with a curate nearby in order to conclude the matter between us to your satisfaction?" she asked, careful to keep her voice low and the tone even. It was necessary for him to show a loss of imperturbability first, and then she could equal any display of ill humor from him. "A swift vow from you, a swifter from me, and you can proceed to your normal pursuits, whatever those might be."

"I discern that you may not be in the best of humors," said his lordship.

"Ah, and there is the deprecating smile that must have enchanted young ladies from your time in the cradle onward," said Pamela without an increase in volume. "It conveys modesty and warmth and manly charm."

Kinnon pursed his lips briefly but then said, "It seems that I have in some way given offense."

"A reasonable conjecture," she conceded.

"Might I know why?"

"You might, and indeed you ought to. But it doesn't appear that you do."

Kinnon said patiently, "I didn't conceive of our meeting to be one in which I would be victimized."

"Then I suggest you cut the meeting short, my lord. It is within your power to do so."

"May I point out that it was not I who wrote out the document which has apparently brought us closer?"

"I beg to disagree with the assumption that

anything whatever would bring me closer to an ancestor-worshiping toady."

Kinnon recollected now that she had made a previous remark about independence, and that one allied to her just concluded peroration was enough to explain belatedly why she felt about him as she did. No peer of the realm, inured to debate at the House of Lords as he was, could possibly have interpreted those words as tokens of friendship.

"You have been outraged at my caution," he said thoughtfully. "Perhaps also by my lack of anxiety to commit myself without further thought to the course you perceive as being correct."

Pamela nodded at this, instead of speaking. She sensed that it wasn't Lloyd Wilcoxen's custom to think aloud in this mode and was moved by the experience.

"But the key to the matter remains that you are enraged, Miss Pamela," he added. Having looked at her so closely, a new note was pervading his speech, it seemed, a note of genuine regret. "In that case, I am certain you will permit me to withdraw."

Pamela's next words passed her lips before she was able to call them back.

"Are you leaving already?"

In part of her mind she had intended to speak sarcastically. Some interference had emerged, however. At the prospect of this handsome man departing from her side, she heard herself sounding vexed and unsettled.

Once again he started to smile but corrected himself at the prospect of renewed criticism from her. It was true enough that his smile was magnetic to women and he used it accordingly, but he didn't conceive that expressing a feeling of interest in a female was by itself at all detestable. He would have been imperceptive, however, not to realize that Miss Pamela didn't entirely loathe him with every fiber of her being.

Pamela, in turn, saw what she perceived as a wicked glint in his eyes. About this, too, she would have liked to speak disparagingly. Refraining was far from easy for her. It seemed obvious that to indulge herself would amount to giving proof that she noticed every feeling as it was conveyed in his mobile features.

"We shall meet again," he said.

As if from a distance, Pamela recollected the original intention to cause a show of anger in him. Never had a female been less successful.

"If I have my way we won't meet."

"Then you can certainly pardon me at this time." His eyes were inviting her to join in the amusement he wouldn't otherwise express. "Indeed I have suddenly recollected the need for an urgent conference relating to matters of concern in the House of Lords."

She was vaguely aware of murmuring voices near her. No doubt many supernumeraries were watching the encounter at which she had failed so signally to provoke him to anger. It did seem, however, as if each of them had been stirred to other and more disconcerting feelings.

Kinnon reached a hand toward one of hers and held it. Despite the pale gloves which custom forced her to wear, Pamela could feel the one hand suddenly turned sensitive up to her shoulder.

When he eased the hand down reluctantly and turned, Pamela drew the first deep breath that had come to her since his appearance. The contact, the speech, the attitudes, all had been as intimate as a kiss observed by a large public. Rarely if ever had the sensible Miss Forrest felt so inexplicably happy and at the same time so outraged.

CHAPTER 4
A Decided Lack of Approval

Had she been alone it would have been the feelings of pleasure that predominated. As it was, aware of others looking at her and still others pointedly looking away but making contact out of the corners of their eyes, feelings of outrage became uppermost.

She had considered, as we have seen, that it would be useful to inflame the pliable Kinnon to a show of anger in public. This goal had not been met. Kinnon's presence, as well as affronting her faculties, had in some way destroyed her will when they had been close and he had been addressing her and none other. It was a response in herself that she had not observed when they had danced together at one occasion in the dim past. At that time she had been aware of being in a rakehell's presence. With increasing age, she had possibly become weakened in her perceptions.

Given the benefit of mature wisdom, she felt certain that if he had remained only a little longer the plan to provoke him into some display of temper would indeed have worked. As he had abruptly departed, however, with an excuse spurred by some awareness of her mixed feelings, the matter could not be tested.

Nonetheless, Miss Pamela Forrest was now determined to obtain redress for the upset he had inflicted upon her.

Keeping that objective firmly in mind, she made the attempt to ignore those who glanced thoughtfully in her general direction. Skillfully she navigated the highly polished floor in an effort to meet with that one person who might be of assistance in this hour of need.

As if on cue, the violinist and pianist suddenly launched into what was supposed to be a *valse* but which would probably have caused a true musician to experience the sort of fit she had been anxious to provoke in his lordship. Her eyes met Aunt Rosemary's only briefly, but her aunt saw that Pamela was proceeding elsewhere and continued speaking with Lady Criddon and some females of similar age and station.

Avery Holt was seated, the position he generally preferred rather than to look down at others from a great distance. An older gentleman was speaking.

"That's what Sir John Conroy told me," the older gentleman was saying, with a brush at his muttonchop whiskers. He was referring to the former equerry to the late Duke of Kent, the man who had helped the widowed Duchess raise the current Queen. " 'As long as she accepts advice from those at her side, which she will do, you may expect her to be a worthy sovereign.' His exact words."

The older gentleman didn't have to add that, upon succeeding to the throne, Victoria had sent Sir John packing.

The Queen had become a bride only last year, now that Pamela recollected, but that didn't mean every woman in the kingdom had to make what others would consider a glittering union. A female was more than a mere convenience to give some male the sons to carry on his line.

Several moments were required for brief introductions, acknowledged gracefully by Pamela and by the whiskerando. The latter, sensing that a consultation of some sort was in the offing, gave the young solicitor a look of envy for being in contact with such an attractive young member of the opposite sex. Avery bore the silent congratulations stoically and waited till the other had lost himself amid the merry throng.

"Pardon me for not rising," he said, perhaps for the hundredth time in addressing Pamela at gatherings of this ilk.

Pamela, absorbed by her own difficulties though she was, felt some pity for this oversized friend of her youth.

"I saw you in conversation with Kinnon a moment ago," Avery said approvingly, thereby forfeiting every ounce of sympathy that had been extended. "It seemed as if the two of you were getting along quite well."

"He was, but I wasn't."

"I am sorry to hear that. Lloyd is an estimable fellow with many good qualities."

"I'm sure that much the same was said about Attila the Hun in his day."

"There can be no possible comparison."

"As the better man, therefore, he will be puzzled by the lawsuit."

"By the—I do beg your pardon!"

"The lawsuit, the action at law if you prefer, which I plan to commence against him."

"Is there a reason for this, or are you motivated by cantankerousness and nothing more?"

"He humiliated me."

"I am not hearing this! If a regiment of Silks were to swear that they have audited your words, I would still have to aver that nothing of what you just said has made the slightest impression upon me."

"It had always seemed to me that your besetting sin is a total lack of imagination," Pamela said, after a brisk shake of her recently coiffed hair. "It seems that I was wrong and perhaps it is only a fear of accepting any responsibility that afflicts you so powerfully."

Avery snorted, almost as if he had been pinked in a duel.

An interruption came in the attractive shape of Lady Suzanne. The daughter of their host and hostess appeared in an aura of pale good looks. Even the scent behind each ear and perhaps on the cleavage was one that would have been worn only by a blonde. A bright redhead like Pamela would have to sport a scent that was heavier and less (no other word would suit) ethereal.

Lady Suzanne's concerns, as they promptly developed, were not ethereal in the least.

"Pammie, I was contented to see you and Kinnon in conversation together." There was a smile on her face, but not one that fattened the cheeks or made eyes look like pellets. "Truly, it pleases me that the two of you have reconciled, so to speak, as it will please all your friends. I trust that the nuptials will take place at St. George's, my dear. Much preferable to Eaton Square."

So abrupt a dismissal of St. Peter's as the venue for a wedding wasn't enough to affect Pamela at all. It took whatever courtesy she could muster, generally considerable, to keep a pleasant demeanor.

Avery, under no such obligation, waved a hand dismissively.

"Wedding? Ha! Quite the contrary. This young lady, your guest, Lady Suzanne, thinks that she has grounds for a lawsuit against Kinnon. She feels that she was humiliated by his presence."

"A jury will understand what I say."

"Not as long as there are no women among the great unpaid," Avery began. This time he raised a hand to show the palm. "I realize that in your view it is not fair that no women are permitted to serve on such a panel, but the point is that they are not. In which case, no such action as you envisage could possibly lie."

Pamela supposed she looked as if the concept was difficult to believe.

"As you find my words unacceptable, I will be

glad to give you a chit to one of my many respected colleagues and let you hear his opinion. I don't know a solicitor who wouldn't listen sympathetically and then shrug his shoulders afterward and talk to others in a pejorative manner about the reasoning powers of women."

At this, Pamela must have frowned massively.

"I should, of course, have said, 'the reasoning powers of some women.' As I was not making a speech, I chose my words with less care than the P.M. when closeted with the Queen."

"Your apology is reluctantly accepted," Pamela said. "In other words, no woman can obtain justice before the bar."

"A moot point," said Avery. He was still stung by the charge that he was chary of accepting responsibility and made every effort to evolve a suggestion upon which a coward like himself could firmly place his professional imprimatur. "If I were you, Pamela (a most unlikely happening, to be sure, but I make the hypothesis to facilitate my communicating this thought), I would seriously consider marrying another and doing it quickly. There is hardly a moment to be lost, it seems to me, if one wants to keep a position among the Fashionables."

" 'Another'?" Pamela recoiled. "Any other

male might be just as thoughtless of a woman's feelings and wishes and, indeed, of her very presence! As we have just seen, I may add."

Avery shrugged. He had performed his duty by offering a suggestion, possibly the first in his life. Discussing objections to it was not a task which he was prepared to accept as well.

"Furthermore, I wouldn't have a dowry for the purpose," she insisted.

Avery, on the point of remarking that Pamela's Aunt Rosemary would surely make some provision for such a development, once again accepted the value of that celebrated apothegm which deals so cogently with the better part of valor.

"I cannot marry another!" she said snappishly. "Indeed I will not!"

With that much made clear, she turned and walked out of earshot.

No doubt she had meant to convey that she would follow no such course until she was ready to do so, but she had spoken what may have been in the deepest recesses of her mind. Although not the most intuitive of mortals, Avery understood that Pamela Forrest was attracted by Kinnon to a greater extent than she would admit. The circumstances bringing them together, as it happened, were enough to prevent her from acknowledging her feelings. He had known Pamela from childhood as someone who felt strongly about many matters but insisted that her feelings were wholly based on rationality and logic. The impact of a Lloyd Wilcoxen upon the mature Pamela, who was thrust into his company by the wishes of a beloved uncle, must be disturbing in the extreme.

As if to confirm that idea, he turned to Lady Suzanne. Before he could make the usual apology for not rising, her eyes had met his.

"There seems to be more here than meets the eye," said Lady Suzanne, conceding without words that she was in total agreement with him.

"Far more," said Avery Holt, Esquire.

The canoe landau drifted in an almost leisurely way from the grassy section of Green Park, pleasantly somnolent on this June morning, and over to the Pall Mall area.

One of the two females in the comfortable seats, however, was seething.

Only the necessity to avoid overstatement compels the sensation-seeking chronicler to aver that Miss Pamela Forrest was seething. Miss Forrest, indeed, was white with anger. The primary cause was an uncertainty as to whether she herself was the object of that anger.

Uppermost in her mind was the wish to see Lloyd Wilcoxen, the Earl of Kinnon, yet again. At this time she did not know whether that wish would be granted. Another talk with him would permit her to make it clear to him (and to herself, although she didn't realize it) exactly how she felt about him. Moreover (although she didn't realize that, either) she would provide herself with an excuse to discover some further obstacle to seeing Kinnon ever afterward, some confirmation that marriage between them must be impossible. Handsome and good-mannered he may have been, but a difficulty should soon present itself to let her thwart the domination of others.

True, he had been a rake in his younger days, but it was possible to argue that his time of adventuring with females would be over after he committed the deed of marriage. The assertion wasn't one that she might dispute. Until she could clearly say what was going to prevent her from being happy as Lady Kinnon, Pamela would be a most unhappy young woman. If the matter wasn't of such overriding importance, she would certainly have smiled at that particular realization.

All this while Aunt Rosemary was speaking serenely about last night's ructions at the Criddon snuggery. As she wasn't able to help alleviate her niece's palpable anguish, she sensibly spoke only of what had been pleasant.

"Truly, I felt as if I had never been away," Aunt Rosemary was saying almost lightly. Her mourning period was definitely in the past, only to be recollected privately on occasion. "I thought that Suzanne was looking very well."

"Indeed she was," Pamela had to agree. This was no time to say that Lady Suzanne Boyce, in her desire to see nuptials between Pamela and the odious one who was supposed to be foisted off upon her, had deserted to the enemy's camp.

Aunt Rosemary sensed a reservation in her niece's tone and changed the subject immediately.

"I see you in a bright lilac," she said almost complacently. "You are bound to look well in it."

Pamela's aunt was always choosing clothes for her. Tear-filled arguments had taken place in Pamela's childhood because aunt insisted on niece wearing dresses of a jarring complexity. In the last years Pamela had come to think that Aunt Rosemary wanted to dress herself, Rosemary, as a younger woman.

Eventually the aunt had been prevailed upon to let Pamela wear simpler dresses. Never was she permitted to wear certain colors, which, she was told, were best suited to the poor. Expressing rebellion as best she could, Pamela had torn out pictures of dresses from various publications and sometimes held the dress pictures in front of a mirror so that she could gain a notion of what they would look like with her features above them. Once in a great while through the onset of young adulthood she had been able to purchase a handkerchief in a pattern that she felt showed her to advantage.

Not for the first time, therefore, it occurred to Pamela that she had been reared by a practical older woman and her husband as well. The serene logic of those people hadn't been transmitted to her, which was most unfortunate. The more practical the choices made in her name, though by people whose love for her was fully returned, the more rebellious she had always found herself becoming.

Indeed she hadn't particularly liked the deep black satin de Lyon under a black cloak that she was wearing now. Aunt Rosemary had insisted on its purchase. No doubt the contrivance showed off her blazing red hair to the greatest possible advantage, but Pamela always felt that she had been maneuvered into accepting the garment along with a panoply of accessories.

"Here we are at last," said Aunt Rosemary contentedly as the landau wheezed to a halt. "What a pleasant duty it has always been, my dear, to form your tastes and be sure that your beauty isn't thrown out on dress or effects that it would be improper for you to wear."

Pamela made some courteous acknowledgment of this well-meant observation.

They were near the fashionable Schomberg House. Mr. Thomas Gainsborough was no longer in residence there, the noted painter having died back in '88 or thereabouts. It did seem, though, that every human who was encountered in these particular precincts reminded Pamela of a portrait by the great artist. Probably it was the look of having been scrubbed and the features whitened to a state of selective bloodlessness.

"I wish that something could be done to reduce the frequency of purchasing coachmen's uniforms," Aunt Rosemary said suddenly, after a casual look at the family retainer who had impassively helped her out of the vehicle. "Fortunes are expended in that cause."

Pamela soon joined her aunt upon terra firma. Both were confronting a building of four stories. Over the entrance was a printed sign: MLLE BLANCHE. No further identification was deemed necessary.

In this assessment, Mlle Blanche (who apparently scorned punctuation as well as further elucidation) was correct. A modiste without compare, as her reputation amply testified, she drew many females to this unlikely place of business in the heart of an area devoted in the main to housing the premises of varied and exclusive gentlemen's clubs. Her services had been performed primarily on behalf of women whose figures deviated from what was customary, but who wanted to look well. Those who were *enceinte* and therefore confined to home quarters were deeply grateful for the rig-outs which Mlle Blanche or her minions constructed to hide the temporary awkwardness. This work on behalf of emotionally beleaguered females had earned her the honorary title of the Galen of the modiste's art.

Pamela felt awkward at the notion of being

attended in a firm whose clients tended to be of diverse shapes. Nonetheless, she had followed her aunt's firm recommendation and was making this exploratory visit.

"Blanche will be delighted to see you," Aunt Rosemary had insisted. "Too many of her patrons are different, so to speak. Confronted with a near beauty, which is exactly what you are whether you credit that or not, Blanche will strain every fiber to achieve perfection."

It was sensible advice, as was only to be expected, but Pamela would rather have been soothed by the ministrations of Miss Prince at the Exeter 'Change or Miss Rebecca in the depths of the Burlington Arcade. However, comfort and contentment were not to be hers for the purchase of the ball gown which had brought her to this place.

The lower floor was pleasantly scented. Women who looked entirely normal proceeded back and forth arranging various purchases. At different counters an eager customer could acquire reticules, beads, Letchford's Perfumes in those cunning three-ounce colored bottles, Hyperion fluid for the growth of hair, Grape Leaf Gin, and the ever recurring bottled frangipani odor.

"The place is a veritable bazaar," she murmured.

"Peace and quiet will reign above," her aunt promised.

She was referring to the floor above rather than to an afterlife, as it soon developed. The conviction was amply justified. Here, the few clerks walked with discretion upon heavily carpeted flooring. No word was spoken above a whisper. The patrons, too, appeared well dressed and many were attractive to the eye. Pamela was much relieved by the sight.

Aunt Rosemary was making it clear that she expected to be dealing with Mlle Blanche and not any underlings. Within moments both were ushered into the presence of a plain-looking woman who spoke with an indubitably British accent, perhaps learned in Sussex at a guess.

Mrs. Sarah Potterton, for that was the owner's true name, listened respectfully to Aunt Rosemary's request for a ball gown of a bright lilac coloring. Experienced in dealing with young and older women in pairs, she made a point of deferring to Pamela as well. It was becoming clear why so many patrons made varied purchases at this lady's emporium.

"The fit will pose no difficulty," said Mrs.

Potterton with a careful and relieved look at Pamela. "It is only a matter of reaching decisions about the various little knobs and curlicues, if any."

By dint of drawings and occasional made-to-order dresses displayed for purposes of comparison, a suitable garment was evolved. This would be of rich silk crossed with darker checkers. Aunt Rosemary wanted it to have side trimmings formed of velvet and mingled with black ornaments.

"I would advise against that," said Mlle Blanche after a glance at Pamela's doubtless expressive features. "Simplicity is on the rise in ball gowns, Mrs. Forrest, and considerable ornamentation will soon be out of style."

Pamela made a note to return to Mlle Blanche's emporium for further additions to her wardrobe as the need arose. Her aunt could hardly offer any objections to such a course.

In the matter of coloring, however, Pamela had to give way. Lilac, rue it or no, did show off the red hair to advantage and helped the eyes with their violet shading, as she thought of them, into the bargain.

The conversation between the two widows wandered to other subjects, and Pamela took advantage of this new development to explore these premises further. Just as she was turning a corner on a room that boasted the largest triptych of mirrors she had ever seen, a panel opened at her left and Miriam Packwood emerged.

Miss Packwood's eyes widened at sight of Pamela and she pulled back briefly as though wounded.

"You!" said Miss Packwood.

"I might say the same." Pamela smiled, her good humor restored by the excessive reaction from a friend.

Miss Packwood's mamma insisted on utilizing Mlle Blanche's services because the daughter was thinner than natural. Blanche or some cohort managed to dress her, however, so that she appeared, if not quite buxom, not undernourished either.

The two girls had often discussed the difficulty of dealing with older women in positions of authority. Lady Packwood not only insisted on accompanying her daughter on such occasions when dental work needed to be done to her, but wouldn't leave the operating chamber and rushed to her daughter's side if Miriam so much as took a deep breath. One result of such ministrations was that Miriam had trained herself to show as little emotion as possible at all occasions.

Miriam Packwood's lapse at this particular moment was therefore a noteworthy event.

"I hardly expected to see you," she said in partial explanation.

Pamela assumed that Miriam was one of those who brought great emotion to the purchase of clothes. Forgetting her own excesses of a few moments ago, she decided upon tolerance of another person's foibles.

"Did your mamma come with you?"

"She is unfortunately indisposed," Miriam said, reminding her friend of something that Pamela had forgotten.

"Pray offer my compliments and best wishes for a speedy recovery."

"Thank you." Miriam in turn remembered her manners. "Is your aunt here?"

"In conference with Mlle Blanche."

"My compliments to her if our paths don't cross today." Further demonstrating her own manners, Miriam said, "That dress you have on now is most attractive."

"Thank you, Miriam. Haven't you seen it before?"

"I'm not certain. Where did you purchase it?"

Pamela spoke about the virtues of Miss Rebecca at the Burlington Arcade.

"I wish *I* could have a choice of modistes," Miriam Packwood said, flushing darkly.

Pamela promptly offered a compliment on her friend's rig-out, which was well received. The encomium came from the heart. Miriam was always nicely turned, thanks to Mlle Blanche. The lady could possibly have caused Avery Holt, Esquire, to resemble a dwarf.

"I am here to arrange for a gown that I can wear to the ball that your mamma and pappa will be giving shortly," Pamela said, fracturing the brief lull that had followed the exchange of compliments about dresses.

"Oh!" For a young woman who rarely showed feelings, Miss Packwood was becoming what her aunt sometimes called a cake-wit. "You mustn't!"

"What do you mean?"

"I shouldn't tell you, but—oh dear, it is best to say the thing and have it done. My pappa feels strongly that you cannot be invited because of your attitude to an elder for whom he had so much respect. Oh, my friend, I *am* sorry!"

Pamela pursed her lips. It was vexing to find herself bereft of an invitation to one social function that would briefly be rated of some importance in the little world of the Fashionables.

"Never mind, then." Only a heart of stone would have been unmoved by Miriam's genuine discomfort. "No difficulties can come between friends."

"I—I don't want them to."

Pamela made a courteous farewell to the other and walked slowly back to the room where Aunt Rosemary and the modiste were in the final throes of their conversation. Rather than tell her aunt that some of the latter's forebodings were indeed coming true, Pamela made a point of smiling warmly.

By way of an apology in part for the recent disturbance she had caused, she said, "I do truly think, dear Aunt, that the color of the new gown represents an excellent choice."

The house in the Brompton Road reflected moonlight on window glass as Pamela and her aunt approached. This engagement to dine had been concluded some months ago. The other day Aunt Rosemary had been granted permission to bring Pamela with her.

"You must not show distress," her aunt counseled urgently as Pamela alighted from the landau. The tale of Miss Packwood's regrets had been communicated in detail, assimilated, and not commented upon. "As far as anyone else knows, all is well with you."

Rather than concede that somehow she happened withal to be in good spirits as long as her thoughts didn't turn to a certain peer, Pamela nodded as if she was bracing herself.

In the ladies' retiring room at the head of the stairs some moments later, Pamela freshened herself with only the most perfunctory look in the mirror. Nor did she accept the ministrations of Charity, the upper housemaid, who had been transported to these premises solely to be of assistance in such matters. Her light coloring would show to advantage. To give herself courage she hadn't really needed, Pamela for once utilized beauty aids that were supposed to enhance skin tones, to soften brittle hair and keep breasts looking slim in silhouette despite their satisfying amplitude. Head erect, eyes front, she descended to the foot of the carpeted stairs.

Aunt Rosemary was in conversation with Lady Marian Woodruff, the hostess, who was apparently under some stress.

"I hope I may see you afterward," Lady Woodruff suggested to Aunt Rosemary. "When the ladies have retired, perhaps you'll allow me a minute to perform a most painful but necessary —ah, yes, as I say."

"Certainly," Aunt Rosemary agreed with notable sangfroid, and turned to greet the night's justly honored lion.

Tonight's guest of honor, holding himself rigidly erect in spite of his seventy-two years, was none other than Arthur Wellesley, the Duke of Wellington himself, the nemesis of Buonaparte, the ladies' man and wit who had dabbled in poetry and statecraft. Pamela had heard, without paying undue attention to the rumor, that he was likely to serve in Sir Robert Peel's Cabinet if Lord Melbourne handed in his resignation as Prime Minister. A well-spoken and courteous man he might have been, but the depthless eyes were not kind. Compassion had been left out of this hero's nature.

"Your most humble and obedient servant," the Duke murmured, and those eyes looked into Pamela's for the first time. She found herself wondering if she would have become a conquest of the Iron Duke's. How might she have responded to a young and handsome Arthur

Wellesley rather than to a Regency rake who had lived so long past his roistering prime?

"Miss Forrest, your name is on the way to becoming a byword," the Duke said mildly, proving that he was still not too busy to keep abreast of gossip.

"Thank you kindly, Your Grace." Pamela was speaking more carefully than usual. "Perhaps a byword for independence of thought."

"Human beings do not value that quality, I fear." The Duke cocked his head thoughtfully. "As long as three persons are together, the one who thinks for himself, right or wrong, will earn the disapproval of the other two."

She was beginning to feel that she had underestimated this shrewd gentleman. He showed a talent for diplomacy of a type that didn't involve relations between different countries or political figures.

"As for marriage, there is much to be said for it," the Duke added quietly while Aunt Rosemary endorsed this sentiment with an approving nod and Pamela wondered if the Duke wanted to make a fine impression upon the older woman, too. "There is the companionship of another and the knowledge that it is possible to give birth legally, so to speak."

Clearly, this High, Puissant, and Most Noble Prince, as he must be styled in heraldic documents, was far too knowledgeable about human nature to be anything but cynical. That a man so perceptive should be popular both for his own person and for his deeds was a great tribute to the upper levels of society.

"And there is something to be said for the knowledge in later years that one has experienced marriage," the old man continued. "I fear that, with the grim reaper snapping at my heels, some variant of the subject of mortality is never far from what remains of my scattered wits. Ah —and here, if I mistake not, is the call for supper. Hardly a moment too soon, in my opinion."

The dining room of Baron and Lady Woodruff boasted simple lighting, with varicolored candles spaced ten feet apart over a wide sturdy table. Pamela soon realized that she and Aunt Rosemary had been given places near the hostess and far from the orbit of the guest of honor. It was no mark of favor, but Aunt Rosemary accepted it stoically.

Pamela's instinct was to question the hostess about this and embarrass her if at all possible. Aunt Rosemary's example kept her quiet. Further, it was impossible not to be delighted by

Wellington's monologue. In the years of what he called his anecdotage, he retailed one incident after another of his color-filled life, stirring the men to admiration and the ladies to round-eyed rapture.

By many standards the meal was light, consisting only of cock-a-leekie soup, a mutton haunch with steamed vegetables, the smoky and steaming Lapsang souchong tea. The Baron was a campaigner against what he called overeating in the upper classes. He felt that laborers alone should eat prodigiously because they would need the strength. Social equals or superiors were invited to his home in order, as was sometimes said, to be tortured.

Pamela wasn't blessed with a strong appetite, as it happened, and approved of crusades even if they seemed based upon wrongheaded premises. She looked dully in front of her at the conclusion of the meal. No sweet was being served, which wasn't entirely surprising.

Lady Woodruff stood. It was accepted that the females would now troop into the sitting room to discuss such topics as the raising of the young and the dissolution of good manners such as had been known in the speakers' best years.

Pamela observed that Aunt Rosemary had

moved off to a corner for a conversation with the hostess. It would have been bad-mannered in the extreme to attempt to gain any knowledge of what was taking place between them until such time as Aunt Rosemary spoke about the matter.

In the meantime the Duchess of Maughan was discoursing about an incident in her girlhood. It seemed that the future Duchess had been determined to learn about painting from that celebrated artist of the day, Mr. Willesdean. She had arranged to take lessons with him as one of a group of five. Certain that her mother would disapprove, the young woman had kept it a secret.

On the second day of lessons, the Duchess said sadly, her mother had rushed into the room and argued with the young girl in the hearing of everyone else. In vain did the tearful young woman say that she wanted only to paint and paint. The mother had insisted upon her "baby's" energies being what she called fresh when the time came for her to be escorted by a possible future husband. The girl had dissolved into tears and run out. Only next day had she written Mr. Willesdean to say unhappily that she had better not come back.

The mother had insisted her act had been inspired only by "my baby's" welfare and purchased a new ball dress to compensate her. In later years, the mother had claimed, her daughter would be thankful because the actions had been taken.

"I felt terrible about it at the time," the Duchess added. "And now *my* oldest daughter, Araminta, wishes to take music lessons with some Italian pianist named Malatesta or Malediction or something. I shall have to adopt firm measures almost immediately. My true punishment for having been recalcitrant as a young girl is that I am put into my mother's position."

Pamela was on the point of taking a strong exception to the older woman's views. The Duchess would be making it far more difficult for another human to experience gratifying discoveries, to find out more about her true nature. The Duchess seemed not to accept the idea that she would be repeating the same injustices that had been practiced upon her!

Before Pamela managed to clear her throat, she saw Aunt Rosemary proceeding in her direction to take part in the various discussions that were now under way as a result of the Duchess' confession. A frown marred Aunt Rosemary's usual unlined features and this once her lips were pursed.

Pamela leaned forward. "Is everything well?"

"Of course, child," Aunt Rosemary said, and only the last word was proof that the older woman was upset. It seemed likely that Pamela's previous actions had been instrumental in causing the difficulty.

Pamela sat restlessly through one of the other ladies' confession that her mother had insisted on traveling through the speaker's childhood, causing her to tell more than one set of recently made friends that she was leaving again. She would do her best to make them jealous of her for going off. The girls always promised to write, but the speaker guessed sadly even then that they'd forget her soon enough.

The speaker added that her widowed mother had certainly tried to keep the daughter away from others. She had wanted the daughter never to acquire friends or to marry but always be living with her, always be dependent on her for everything. An apoplectic stroke had kept the mother's plan from reaching fruition. Just before the mother's coffin was going to be lowered into cold earth, however, the daughter had insisted it be opened once more so that she could kiss her for the last time.

"I have often wondered whether I was thanking her for everything she had done for me before dying or for—even after all these years I cannot bring myself to say it, but I have often wondered all the same."

Any male auditor would have been astonished and dismayed to know that women would speak in such terms at any time, and especially after a pleasant supper in which everyone had seemed in good spirits.

Only by the greatest exercise of will did Pamela refrain from making a contribution to the symposium which was developing. Aunt Rosemary, having discerned that the topic dealt with matters in the past for which no redress was possible, had turned to another listener her own age and begun to talk quietly about the new fashion for sleeves that were shorter than arm's length. To Pamela's surprise, the response was warm and fervent.

The festivities, if such they could be called, drew to a close at last. Courtesies were exchanged before departure. Pamela overheard her aunt offering their hostess that exact measure of deference required by custom but not a whit more. No greater conclusive proof could have been found that Aunt Rosemary was upset.

Driving home by the Brompton Road, with its low-to-the-ground homes that always reminded Pamela of the cemetery land in which victims of the cholera epidemic of '32 were buried, she saw the pensive look on her aunt's features.

"You are going to tell me that nothing was wrong between you and the Baroness," Pamela said. "I am not prepared to believe that."

"My dear," Aunt Rosemary began, and then spoke thoughts which seemed beside the point. "There are always scandals about the treatment of the poor at workhouses, but nothing is ever changed. The poor live in agony while others are told only about recent discoveries and luxuries which people like us and none others are able to afford."

Pamela was far from surprised by this apparent diversion. Together with a number of other women whose status would keep them from poverty forever, Aunt Rosemary served on a committee that was intended to be of aid to the poor of London.

"It is a national problem," Aunt Rosemary insisted, her gloved fingers clenched. "An Empire-wide problem, to be sure. There are rustic families in which the children eat flour and butter with water poured over it and their supper is one piece of bread, sometimes with cheese but more often not. Supper for those who are more fortunate may consist of bread and potatoes. The only meat that passes some of their lips at all is on Saturday, when they might have bacon. But no excuse is possible for such things taking place all around the Empire, no excuse for not offering far more aid."

"I am in agreement with what you say, Aunt, to be sure, but I do not know what effect this has upon my initial question."

Aunt Rosemary, spurred by that interjection, gathered her forces to speak directly to the point.

"You are aware that the Baroness, or Lady Woodruff as she prefers to be called, under the delusion that she will be mistaken for the wife of an Earl, perhaps, is in charge of a charity which aids a certain segment of the London poor."

"Yes." Pamela searched her memory. "The Fund for Fallen Women, I believe."

Aunt Rosemary nodded.

"It sounds as if they had physically dropped

from a height," Pamela said, and immediately regretted the impulse to relieve her aunt's palpable unhappiness, if only for a moment. Rosemary Forrest had experienced so much difficulty in these last months that an additional awkwardness for her seemed damnable indeed!

"You are an aide-de-camp of the Baroness' in that cause, I believe," she said quickly to make up for the well-intended *gaffe.*

"Not any longer," Aunt Rosemary said, and no one who knew her less well than Pamela would have guessed at the bitterness behind those even tones. "Not as of tonight. The fallen women may have the children out of wedlock without my having to stir myself to take the interest that they deserve."

"Then you mean that you are no longer germane to the issue," Pamela began brightly, and wanted to bite off her tongue for once again indulging in levity that had actually been well meant but was inappropriate. She spoke next with the seriousness that the subject truly deserved. "You have been dismissed?"

"The dear ·Baroness prefers to call it an earned *congé* agreed upon between herself and the other ladies."

"But you have worked harder for the cause

than any of them and they must all know it!" Pamela protested, fully aroused now. "Why should any of them want to send you packing unless it is because your efforts put them all to shame, every one?"

But she had already deduced the entire reason before the landau rolled onto Cromwell Road, that elegant street which had been named after the son of the Protector.

Aunt Rosemary, not aware of the speed with which Pamela's mental processes had adapted on this occasion, added, "I have been clearly told that it is felt that I raised a child who is deficient in obeying her elders, and therefore I would create an unfortunate example to the young women I am supposed to aid and guide. My service, in other words, would be a liability."

Pamela knew better than to apologize once more because of what she had indirectly wrought. She still felt guiltless of error, and her aunt knew very well that Pamela would have spared her the least pain had it been at all possible.

"I hope you can keep from letting yourself be upset for a long time over this."

Aunt Rosemary nodded once, instead of giving her usual emphatic nod when something was said with which she fervently agreed.

This was the time to be cheerful, Pamela felt. "Indeed, if I had been given what is actually a merciful release, I would strike back at my would-be tormentors."

"And how do you suggest I do that?"

"By founding another charity of my own and not letting any of the witches take part of it." With a recollection of the confessions she and others had listened to, Pamela added, "Some charity to aid the children of wealthy parents."

She didn't know whether the observation had been entirely humorous, but Aunt Rosemary chose to accept it in that light.

"We could give those children occasional trips to Bermondsey and the docks, I presume." She grinned. "And frequent improving lectures about morals, to which the poor are so often exposed, would do no harm in the other cases, either."

Pamela smiled in return, not saying that it had crossed her mind only too late that there was more to be said for such a course than considering it as an outlet for exaggeration or malice. She despaired of ever making the point plain, let alone having it accepted. Aunt Rosemary had, after all, raised one niece in comfortable circumstances and was still *in loco parentis* to a nephew, Pamela's brother.

"A charming thought," Aunt Rosemary said in summation. "Not useful, but it is agreeable to contemplate the reactions of elders."

Pamela subsided into silence.

"In my judgment, however," Aunt Rosemary proceeded, "we are not bereft of resources, you and I and even your brother."

"How do you mean?"

"When a crisis emerges during a summer month," Aunt Rosemary said portentously, "there is a course open to us, my dear."

CHAPTER 5
The Pleasures of Outer Darkness

The next day limped past. Preparations to take a summer sojourn were set in motion. On the next day the procession started out with all the *élan* of Crusaders leaving the battlefield after a lively disagreement with a group of infidels.

Pamela, disappointed at not having seen Kinnon at least once more so as to confirm her dislike for him, as she thought of it, felt that the soldiers in this exodus were certainly equipped as well as might be. The canoe landau carried herself and her aunt as well as her young brother. Behind them, in a row of largely borrowed equipment, nestled nearly all of the domestic staff. Two footmen were in the traveling hospital, as it was called, with various patent nostrums collectively weighing almost as much as the canoe landau in front. There was a post chaise holding the cook and Ian's tutor, and a curricle with two footmen and flat wooden chests weighed down with dinnerware.

Two and a half hours away from Canterbury, the goal came into sight.

The well-known resort of Worthsea, where every prospect pleases, was populated by natives who would one and all pause at various times during the day, then look toward Dover and sigh. The volume of sound that they made was optional, but the gesture seemed compulsory. It was a village-wide *tic douleureux,* as a London wit had pointed out, causing a friend to ask waspishly what the devil he was talking about.

The unhappiness in question was caused by the existence of the village of Margate, to the south, and the latter's acceptance far and wide as the primary seaside resort in Kent for London Fashionables during the summer. Worthsea's clientele, select though it may have been, was smaller in volume.

It was the injustice that rankled with natives of all ages. Worthsea boasted twelve miles of sea front, unlike Margate's nine. Along this area, again as in Margate, were placed a grand promenade, a concert pavilion, and various structures intended to offer relief from a scorching sun that never seemed to materialize in Margate. The church of St. Thomas could be viewed by those desiring to improve themselves with an examination of architecture dating back to the times of the Normans. The church could also be attended by some select few who wanted to ingratiate themselves with a Power more awesome even than Victoria's at Windsor.

And yet it was to Margate that most, if not all, of the London Fashionables repaired. As has been said, the injustice rankled. It made Worthsea residents sound cross, which in itself aided the migration to the south a little more than might have been the case otherwise.

"The arrival of this caravan," as Aunt Rosemary said to a bemused young Ian, "will represent a bit of show for the locals."

To spend the month of June, Aunt Rosemary had engaged a cottage that looked over hedges and boasted a low thatched roof. Inside, the walls were whitewashed. In Pamela's view, the furnishings thus displayed more brightly were entirely hideous. No eye could rest when confronted with Belleek porcelain clocks and swan-shaped dishes, acanthus card tables or mahogany side chairs. The prize was a sofa with inverted cornucopias and winged-lion paws for feet. This latter was almost certainly considered a height of elegance in the provinces. Neither

Pamela nor her aunt felt a moment's envy of the true owner of these premises.

One other feature of the establishment was well worth noting. In a sitting-room chair that might have been comfortable only when it was first made sat Lloyd Wilcoxen, the Earl of Kinnon.

The malefactor surged to his feet. Seeing the handsome peer groomed and dressed in the height of fashion for the male, Pamela realized that she hadn't yet escaped the clutches of her traveling clothes, which were colored a deep lavender to hide dust from the road and looked as if they'd been worn for days rather than hours.

Aunt Rosemary, after a courteous inclination of the head, looked at Pamela's doubtless reddening features. "I shall, of course, leave you two and accept it as an article of faith that the door will be kept open."

"My word on it, ma'am."

Alarmed, Pamela wanted to call out that being alone with him offered a dismaying outlook. Words, however, would not come to her dry throat.

"I am surprised that you want to see me," Pamela said as soon as Aunt Rosemary was out of earshot. "By now, you would face the disapproval of society if marriage was planned between you and a pariah such as I have become."

"That is nothing to me." He gave a preoccupied smile, having listened to only a few words. Those now intense gray eyes were curtained, the hands clenching and unclenching as if to warn himself about the necessity of maintaining the courtesies.

She spoke with all the quickness at her command. "Have you come, then, to glory in the sight of my exile and my aunt's?"

"Certainly not."

She was impressed by that firmness in spite of herself. An alarm seemed to be sounding deep inside her.

"Am I, then, being unfair to ask why you have favored my aunt and myself with an appearance at this time?"

"No, quite the contrary, not at all unfair. I have taken time out from Parliament in the midst of a crisis, coming down here by a path I know in which hours can be saved—"

Disappointment flattened her tones. "Indeed!" Apparently he wanted to prove how quickly he could travel, like those sport riders of Aunt Rosemary's youth.

"I have come to assist," he said, "in easing your burden."

She found herself hoping he would want to remain for a while. The impulse to find faults in him had faded. He was pertinacious, not a man easily daunted. Had he wanted to make a mark of his own in life, he would certainly have done so.

"And how, my lord, do you propose to accomplish that worthy goal?"

"By making certain that you see more of me."

A thrill of pleasure racked her at the same time that she told herself she had already seen far too much of him. Words that would effectively dampen his enthusiasm, if such it was, seemed unavailable to her keen intelligence. Never before had she dealt with a male who refused to admit that he had been denied her friendship.

"We have to be seen in public," Kinnon proceeded. "Of course, there will be a servant riding back and forth with us. Indeed your aunt could act as a chaperone if she is willing to do so."

"Or Lord Melbourne could, considering that he will probably have much time to spare in the immediate future." Calculatedly she had re-marked that Melbourne would almost certainly be resigning as Victoria's First Minister. Such a reference coming from a woman was likely to put his lordship off balance, briefly at least.

"My point, as you surely realize," said Kinnon imperturbably, drawing a step closer as if he thought her hearing was impaired, "is that you are seen to be considering the prospect of mar-riage as prescribed for you. It will make a better impression upon the influential ones in society, as I am sure you realize."

"I have no wish to consider such a matter." How could she stop herself from cocking her head coquettishly, as if amused and pleased by the thoughtfulness he was palpably showing? "I hope to clarify it to the meanest intelligence—and there must be few intelligences meaner than those of the Fashionables—that I strongly disapprove of an attempt to order my life be-cause I am a weak woman."

Kinnon refrained from making the point that his own life would be ordered as well. Pamela, looking attentively at the handsome and digni-fied peer, couldn't help feeling that it would have been gratifying to meet him after a long lull, to make his further acquaintance as one

male in a field of many. Instead, she was a creature trapped like a fly in amber, imprisoned by
the recent past.

Kinnon's smile had distressed her at their previous meeting, but she found herself warming to
it now.

"In that case, I suggest a *modus vivendi*, Miss
Pamela. We can be seen together at various
public functions and we will continually explain
how strongly we disapprove of the directive that
your late uncle issued with the connivance of
my late father."

Only by dint of an internal struggle did she
refrain from laughing at the image he had conjured up.

"That is *not* amusing!"

Most likely he had seen the twitching of her
lips. When next his lordship spoke, it was with
renewed confidence.

"If you decide against consorting with me, I
shall follow you everywhere," Kinnon said. "I
shall dog your steps without mercy."

She had to look away briefly, to keep him
from observing the outward manifestations of
her response.

"And when I face you again, I will certainly
not be able to stop myself from doing—this!"

He had taken two steps closer. She looked back at him just after he glanced out the door to make certain that no one was observing his next move.

She felt his lips on hers. The impulse to raise both hands and strike him was present, but only briefly. To her own surprise, she found herself returning the pressure.

It was Kinnon who disengaged himself, albeit reluctantly and slowly.

"I shall next call for you on Saturday, the day after tomorrow, at noon, by which time you should be settled in."

So saying, he strode to the door.

Pamela, looking after him, wondered why she seemed unable to enforce the decision that was correct, the decision to scorn a young man who refused to speak up for his own right to make the choice he wanted. After all, her decision not to involve herself with him was logical. It represented the height of good sense.

To give herself more time to consider this matter, she suddenly sat down upon the abominable sofa. For some reason she was entirely at a loss to understand, her knees were shaking.

CHAPTER 6
A Leman in the Garden of Love

Twelve-year-old Ian Forrest looked up at Aunt Rosemary with his late father's sharp eyes. "Will Pamela be too busy to visit my birthday party?"

"Certainly not," Aunt Rosemary replied. To take the boy's mind off his sister's possible dereliction, caused by a flurry of solitude after yesterday's travel and the Earl of Kinnon's unexpected visit, she added briskly, "As you are going to entertain some of your little friends who are visiting Worthsea and Margate for the summer, you will have to be clean for the occasion."

She rang the silver bell at her side. After a pause, the parlor door opened on a squarely built young girl with a vacant smile.

"Hope, please draw a hip bath for Master Ian." There was a Charity in the household as well, a conjunction which had caused Pamela to point out wryly that there was no Faith among the staff.

"It is done," said Hope.

Despite the name, she was Prussian by ancestry and had been hired in the main because every woman of position nowadays was expected to have a Prussian maid. Such an ornament to the household was circumstantial proof that the family was at least aware of the influence of Victoria's handsome Prince Consort. Not for a moment was it easy to issue orders to some of these imposing domestics, but Aunt Rosemary could bring it off every time. She simply reminded herself beforehand that she and none other was the mistress of the establishment.

Ian let out his breath, conveying that he took the matter of a bath very seriously, as he did so many things. Looking at him in affectionate desperation, Aunt Rosemary wondered about the strange lad who always questioned himself and the responses of others, dealing cautiously with everyone. How was it possible for two such impetuous persons as his and Pamela's elders to have created someone of his nature, a serious dwarf who was betraying their temperaments while subtly reshaping his father's features?

One result of the lad's overwhelming caution was that he found himself with few playmates. Her own purchases of gifts galore never quite served to reassure this lad of good fortune or give him the happiness that ought to have been shining from his features.

Drawing herself up, Aunt Rosemary walked with him to the door. "Be very careful with everything, Hope."

"Yes, mum." The maid recalled that she had been urged to adopt Germanic phrases when possible, though she knew few of them. "*Jawohl*, mum, I meant."

Aunt Rosemary nodded. It was necessary to remind everyone on the staff that many mishaps could occur in this large rented house with its dining room and sitting rooms, parlor, library, and upstairs—not to mention those chambers that were being left unused.

In the kitchen Mrs. Chamberlain, the cook, was grumbling about the man-sized ice container in front of her ample presence.

"Nonsense food," she said sternly, no doubt convinced that a *klutmagar* in Poona wouldn't have accepted the ingesting of hokeypokey in June or any other time. Having worked for a British family in India, the Scotswoman tried to live by her notion of their standards and judged all else accordingly. Rosemary Forrest was shrewd enough to accept the woman's loyalty and make little jokes to Pamela about their cook's prejudices.

She made sure that everything was going well and walked upstairs to the boy's room. Deftly she avoided tripping over Gaiter, the family bulldog, still disconcerted by the change of locale in which to pursue his own activities. Half a dozen pats on the head offered some small comfort in his hour of need.

A small table had been set out with ten places for the young guests at Ian's birthday party. Everything looked fine.

Aunt Rosemary was taking out her knitting needles and oriental gray berlin wool down in the parlor when the rear doorbell rang and brief greetings were exchanged. One or more of the young guests had certainly arrived. The doorbell rang again at ten minutes past four by the Madeleine clock she had brought, and after the inevitable greetings there was an almost complete silence at the door.

Disturbed, Aunt Rosemary made her way upstairs. Not entirely to her surprise, she found Pamela at the boy's door and looking in. With a glance over one shoulder, Aunt Rosemary saw that one boy and one girl were playing a game with Ian, who was dutifully entertaining the only young guests who had been allowed to accept invitations to his party.

There was more commotion at the servants' entrance at six-thirty, but a brief flicker of hope soon died away. The guests' family help had arrived to return those two children to their homes.

Aunt Rosemary, ensconced with her niece in the small sitting room, said, "I shall ask Mr. Gernald to join Ian and offer some consolation. A tutor is equipped for a mission along those lines."

"Not on this occasion." Pamela, rising to her feet, was calm. "Ian has suffered because of my independence, Aunt. It behooves me to go in and speak with him."

Rosemary Forrest wasn't one to deny the truth of a situation that was causing immediate difficulties.

"It is your place to do so, yes," she agreed.

The birthday boy was sitting quietly in his room, flushing under the baleful glare of the green lory bird that he had received among other gifts. Gaiter, who seemed to accept the smaller animal, joined Pamela for this meeting.

"The hokeypokey will last for two days at least," Pamela began, feigning good cheer. "We must not tell Aunt Rosemary, however, or she will want it all for herself."

"Yes," Ian agreed, courteous and formal. "It was really a very nice party. Very nice."

To show warm approval of his good manners would only distract the boy. Taking the discomfited lad into her arms, Pamela kissed him on the forehead and then on the right cheek.

"Happy birthday, darling Ian, and may you be happy on many, many more."

"Thank you," said Ian Forrest tonelessly.

It was into this household, rife with unhappiness from every member of the small family, that the devil-may-care Earl of Kinnon ventured on the next afternoon precisely at twelve o'clock.

He was aware of a woman's eyes following his progress toward the large sitting room but saw Pamela's Aunt Rosemary only when she leaned forward on the sofa she occupied. Seen more closely, Rosemary Forrest looked to be in her forties. Once vivid hair had been darkened by age and wisely kept that way. Her eyes were rather more closely set than was proper for true attractiveness in a woman, but the chin was forceful and interesting in a woman her age.

Dressed to the nines in a polonaise with the black lace insertion cunningly chosen to show a slim midriff and shirred sleeve ruffles to hint at slender arms, the vivid woman in her vivid clothes surveyed his lordship. Kinnon wished as if he didn't feel that a cat's claws were poised for being raked along his chest.

"Your lordship, we can dispense with the initial diplomatic maneuvers, I believe." The cool voice didn't hide purposiveness, or glory in it, either. "You wish to see my niece, as I understand it."

"Yes."

"If you are thwarted, will you leave her alone from that time on?"

"Only for a brief day or so."

"Would you alter that perception if some political advancement were to come your way? It would then be inadvisable to concern yourself with a pariah any longer."

"I have no reason to think that I would change my course."

"Do you wish to marry Pamela?"

The truth was mighty and should prevail. "I cannot even be absolutely certain of that, but I think that she and I can soon decide this matter between us."

Aunt Rosemary couldn't help shutting her eyes tightly and imagining his lordship as a nephew-in-law. He was a handsome and bright man, if not easy to know or to put into any category. Pamela's judgment would have to prevail in this matter. Raising children was a process of easing the yoke of authority a little further again and again until those children were mature.

"You cannot be faulted for plain speech or for unhandsomeness either, to be brutally honest."

Kinnon mustered a smile. "When my late father was not attempting to rearrange my life he sometimes said to me that the shortest paths make for the least tired travelers."

"I am sure that is so. Then you feel that you could make Pamela a good husband?"

"I do indeed."

"I should tell you that her position in society might never be improved from the nadir it seems to have currently reached."

"I accept the possibility."

"And even if she is once more *persona grata*, which may be delayed because of her palpable threshing in the net, so to say, Pamela would not be one of those la-di-da wives whose spines come from Mlle Blanche."

Kinnon was not cognizant of the exact reference but understood its import. He nodded. Certainly Pamela wouldn't come to any discussion with prejudices formed in a silk-lined cradle, at a presentation at court, a cotillion, a society wedding or funeral.

"Your life would be simpler, as you must appreciate, were you to plight your troth with a flibbertigibbet."

Again he realized that a time for truth had arrived. "I would then experience difficulties of another sort. No one is put on earth to live a simple and happy life without pains."

"I must accept your point of view on that aspect of the discussion." Mrs. Forrest's head was erect. Respect had been won at the expense of amiability. She was, almost, like a woman addressing someone equal in age. "I wonder if you can freely discuss another point with me, and then the inquisition will be done."

"I can try."

"That is almost good enough. I must assume that you have at some time in your life had the experience of carnal relations with a woman— no, please do not consider that I create a difficulty for any but the most serious of reasons."

"I have known women, yes."

"Another query, then, and one which may appear an even greater insult." Rosemary Forrest looked around swiftly at the ill-chosen furnishings of this room, which could never before have been present at such a frank conversation between one of each sex and disparate ages. "I ask you to believe in its importance. If by any chance you cannot bring yourself to answer directly, then perhaps you can find some pantomimic way in which to indicate the nature and quality of the response."

"My curiosity is certainly aroused." Kinnon spoke almost as if he were a detached onlooker and his happiness with a chosen woman might not depend on the next few moments of discourse.

"Very well, then. You tell me that you have had carnal knowledge of women. My question, then, is simply this: do you enjoy being with a female?"

"I beg your pardon!"

The breathtaking audacity of that query almost took his faltering breath entirely away. Important to him as the questioner had become, he found it difficult to frame a temperate reply.

"It might be more accurate, your lordship, to ask whether or not you relish their company no matter what activity you may both be occupying yourselves at."

The position was clear. A response had to be made without drawing away from the truth.

"That depends upon the woman."

"But there have been some that you liked? Not just liked 'in their place,' as some foolish members of your sex have been known to say with a snigger."

"That is correct, ma'am."

"I feel, as you surely realize, that my niece has unmistakably proved herself in these last days to be an unusual person. Consequently the male with whom she makes a life must himself enjoy and relish and thrive upon her company."

He had already given the clearest possible answer in these astonishing circumstances, and what had been only hinted must certainly be understood by now.

"*I* feel, then, that the inquisition, as you called our conversation, is a reasonable one."

"Good. I cannot ever sympathize with someone who would leap full tilt at conclusions about me that have not been justified."

"Do you have any other feelings in this matter that should be communicated to me?" It was best, for once, to be blessedly direct. The society in which he lived had forced him into deviousness to obtain what he wanted.

"Primarily that you may be a person with some capacity to show warmth and even to make sacrifices if needed. You could therefore be of great benefit to my niece. And she to you, as goes without emphasizing."

"Then I take it that I have passed the examination with flying colors."

"Oh yes." Mrs. Forrest stood gracefully. "A woman has to do the best she can in order to be of assistance to her nearest and dearest."

In the silence that followed as she drew herself together, he took the liberty of glancing around the room as if Pamela was to be discerned within these four walls. Mrs. Forrest's insistence on frankness had alone caused him to let his impatience show.

That lady, however, smiled. "I will speak in your favor to my niece, of course. But any decisions regarding your lordship are hers to make and hers only. She has earned the right to do so."

"I appreciate your good intentions toward me."

"Thank you. I can now inform Pamela that you await, and make it clear that I think she should descend to join you and offer such courtesies to you as she is now capable of showing."

Young Ian appeared during the following moments. He confined himself to staring up at the older man. Kinnon, normally self-possessed, imagined himself being accused of nameless violations against Miss Forrest. After a tentative smile he looked toward the door from which he anticipated that the maiden would make an appearance.

His expectation was soon justified. Pamela, in a gray walking dress that looked to the casual eye as if it had been engineered during his wait, offered nothing more than a look of appraisal.

"As you see, I have arrived," he began confidently. "My Rawlins awaits."

Ian, listening, seemed suitably impressed at this reference to a vehicle built by the celebrated carriage maker in London's environs.

"I am hardly dressed."

"A cloak will be sufficient in addition to what you now have," he said.

"But no servant is available at this time to act as chaperone."

Kinnon didn't dispute that. Instead he turned to Aunt Rosemary, who came into the room to

take Master Ian by the hand and surgically ex-
cise him from the immediate premises.

"Ma'am, I wonder if we could prevail upon
you to release a female member of your staff for
two or three hours."

Pamela looked up irritably at this man who
had broken many a female heart, to be sure, and
might have done so to hers, as well. At no time
had he hinted in thought or deed that she was
tampering with the truth. Handsome enough,
this devil-may-care peer, but craven in the presence of others and considering, no doubt, that
he was practicing impeccable manners.

Aunt Rosemary, faced by this request, betrayed her niece. "I believe that Charity can be
released from her duties for a few hours."

Disdaining to plead that she suffered an indis-
position, Pamela placed another obstacle in the
path of an afternoon's courtship from this
source.

"I wonder if my brother might accompany
us."

Kinnon looked somewhat less than deliriously
happy at the prospect of spending time in the
company of the grave-faced Ian.

"My brother spent a very difficult day yesterday, and a pleasant journey about the country-

side will surely do him more good than purging with salts."

"I would hope so!" Confronted by such a choice, the generous Kinnon didn't hesitate. "Let us all leave for a time in which we may come to know each other a little better."

But she felt that she already knew him well enough. He had spoken of accompanying Pamela to social functions but was not now committing that brazen act if he ever would. Certainly he was handsome, good-mannered, intelligent, and accommodating. But he gave in to the slightest opposition as well as the most influential. As far as Pamela was concerned at this time, she had already come to know the Earl of Kinnon as well as necessary or desirable.

CHAPTER 7
A Wedding and a Departure

With the serious boy in their company, it seemed that Kinnon felt a twinge of guilt if he so much as smiled. For which reason, he very sensibly engaged himself to cheer up Pamela's brother.

Ian's only interest at first was inclined to revolve around the expensive brougham and its various impedimenta. Kinnon, rather than admit he didn't know the answers, promised that Ian would be permitted later on to consult with the coachman and addressed his efforts to changing the subject.

It soon developed that Ian's interest in such national leaders as Sir Robert Peel and even the semi-inactive Duke of Wellington was only lukewarm. On the way through the village itself, Kinnon paused to buy the lad a thaumatrope disc, thinking that Ian would surely find himself beguiled by the device. He ought to have known better. Ian simply explained in needless detail how it was that, when the disc was spun, the answer to a riddle printed on one side was certain to appear.

"You have clarified a matter that puzzled me for many years," the Earl said gravely.

Pamela, seated near her brother, found herself taking his side. "As I told you previously, your lordship, Ian has recently had a difficult incident inflicted, so to speak, upon him."

Kinnon, rather than point out that somewhat the same experience was occurring to him, gestured for a news dealer at the nearby kiosk to approach with a tabloid newspaper. This he purchased, adding a comfortable amount to the stipend. In the pause it was possible to hear Kinnon's coachman being heavily facetious while he spoke with Charity, who rode at his side.

"Here is the *Penny Intelligencer,*" said the peer, having noted an ample number of illustrations on the first page. "It ought to be easily comprehended and can do nothing but improve your mind even further."

The vexatious Miss Forrest said sternly, "You cannot insist that he read in a moving vehicle."

"We are not now in motion," the Earl began.

Ian resolved the difficulty by beginning to devour the contents as the carriage got under way. Unfortunately he chose to impart his knowledge aloud as he acquired it, and his interest was drawn only to those accounts in which bloodshed was a prominent feature.

"This fellow in Blackheath—do you know what he did? Chopped up his wife and put the remains into a pan of porridge for the children."

"You have certainly helped Ian to gain a deeper knowledge of the world," Pamela said, her voice turning into a suitable imitation of a thundercloud in full eruption. "Give me that paper!"

Ian clutched it to hisself, reveling, no doubt, in the printed communication with a world of distant adults.

It was Kinnon who solved the dilemma, reaching for the paper and folding it in half before easing it to the carpeted flooring.

"I'm taking you to a party," he said pacifically. "You'll not want such a distraction there."

"Not another party," Ian said softly, eyes clouding.

"Every celebration isn't difficult," Kinnon said as the carriage started up yet again. Though unaware of yesterday's sad events, he was responding instantly to the child's mood.

Ian lowered his eyes in unspoken disagreement.

"Young man, you will either have an army commission purchased for you later in life—you could be of that ilk—or discover religion and turn into a pale pink curate, as in the celebrated song. I don't think you'll become one of nature's subordinates, although the process of raising young men for some leader to command proceeds all around us and has social utility. No, you will probably become a leader and an outcast."

Pamela, convinced that the Earl had spoken seriously, asked, "Would you make my brother some sort of a *philosophe?*"

"I believe that Monsieur Voltaire was considered a leading light," Kinnon answered smoothly.

Pamela felt certain that he had only resorted to flippancy in order to evade the slightest of social challenges. She settled back, angry but wordless.

Kinnon pursed his lips, aware that he had somehow lost a chance for pleasanter communication with Miss Forrest. It may have dismayed her that he could see quite so many sides to a given question.

Rarely did he feel at even a momentary loss

for something to say. In this crisis he made a point of looking out the window.

"There!" said Ian suddenly, his eyes having followed Kinnon's except that he was now peering in a different direction. "That must be the party you meant."

In front of a three-story building was a tree-shaped garden infested by men and women smiling happily as they moved around. It happened to be a perfect June afternoon, worthy of this village or of Margate itself. The sun shone benevolently upon the apple-cheeked villagers, some of whom looked better dressed than normal for the denizens of this area as Kinnon had seen them. The Earl, who was no more anxious to witness revelry among strangers than Ian himself, shrugged and looked away.

Pamela, knowing only that Ian's interest might be captured no matter how low his spirits, unwittingly added fuel to this fire.

"I'm sure that many boys and girls are present," she said, thinking that Kinnon may have actually intended to bring them out here. She asked the discomfited peer, "Will you order the carriage to halt, now?"

"As soon as Scruggs finds where the other carriages are, he will do so."

Pamela said reasonably, "Surely he could be prevailed upon to let us off before that."

Kinnon was unsure whether she knew that he was a victim of his own willingness to temporize.

Only at this juncture, when his lordship looked out the window once more to gain time before replying, did circumstances begin to favor him. And then it was a modified turn for the better that took place in his affairs.

The carriage was moving slowly in the presence of so many groundlings. An elder who was dressed to his affordable limits turned and saw Kinnon. He smiled with pleasure.

"Your lordship! You *did* come to my son's wedding! I am honored!"

Kinnon, at a loss to recollect a name, could only conjecture that he had said something courteous to this middle-class gentleman at some time in London. The words had been recollected at this crisis, offering an inducement for keeping up good relations with all whenever that might be possible.

There was no choice now about staying. The carriage halted at Kinnon's signal to the coachman. An awkward Ian descended with Pamela. Kinnon brought up the rear.

"We can stay only for a few minutes," he began.

"My wife and I, we would be honored to have you spend as much of the day as possible with us," the man beamed. "And you know, sir, it's the bride's side as pays for these ructions and I'm happy to give 'em the extra expense."

Kinnon nodded weakly. "We'll walk about and forage for ourselves, thank you very much."

The groom's father sent a small boy to notify other important adults that a peer and friends had come to honor the families. He then turned to the stiffly dressed and uncomfortable young man who had approached, and whose resemblance to the other, allied with the nattiness of his dark clothes, made it plain that it had to be the groom.

Kinnon observed that a number of very young ladies strolled the area, and so did several boys. Ian ought certainly to have been interested but seemed unwilling to join the others. Perhaps they were uncomfortable, too, at being on their best behavior.

Pamela, whose examination of the Earl's mobile features in the last minutes had convinced her that the Earl was as surprised by this occasion as she herself, offered a sardonic smile.

"You seem to have procrastinated your way into a happy concatenation of circumstances."

"He who hesitates is saved," Kinnon answered sententiously, with a grin that wasn't returned.

As he was well aware that Ian remained unhappy, it became clear to Kinnon that, if something could be done to cheer the lad, his sister's gratitude would be helpful in setting a firmer seal on his relations with her.

The father, with his son in tow, spoke loudly to him. "I want you to realize that you must help Glenda build a family. Because of all the trouble you've given your own parents we demand the pleasure of knowing that you, too, will suffer the anguish of having children. And you must be loyal to your wife, as you and Glenda are one now, for all practical purposes. Loyalty is a vital ingredient."

The groom's mother suddenly spoke up. "Loyalty, yes, son, but if any of Glenda's brothers ever come to you and want jobs or some preferment because you are related to them by marriage, well, lad, you do not have to hire anybody for such a foolish reason as that. You must not harm your business affairs because of some harum-scarum accident of nature. Of course I make an exception of Oswald because he is your brother by blood, and blood is thicker than—"

Pamela found herself exchanging warm smiles with Kinnon for the first time. The humorous inconsistencies of parents would alter nothing for long, however, while Ian remained dismally unhappy. His sullenness made it impossible for his escorts to behave like a normal young man and woman.

The bride, Glenda, was talking roguishly to one of the local lads who had been a beau of hers in the past. She was wearing an organdy trimmed with vermicella lace, and it may have cost a fortune but looked on her like a readymade. Nonetheless, the duckling seemed to be making conquests as she moved around, possibly for the one time in her life when they would be of no help to her. Glancing at Kinnon's face with a feeling she could not easily have defined, Pamela thought that his lordship was bemused and no more.

It became impossible to avoid partaking of the dinner. Only Ian failed to muster the required *bonhomie.* Pamela and Kinnon were otherwise within an ace of enjoying themselves and the entire occasion.

The dinner was a memorable one. Kinnon,

with Pamela and Ian as well, sat by the groom's side at a gilt-burnished mahogany table. The peer ate methodically, finishing everything put before him: cream of onion soup, overdone capons with sea kale, oyster patties that seemed to have been scalded, a large and unexceptionable glacé cake, and thick strong tea that was the best-prepared food put before him. He was evidently one of those men gifted by a capricious Providence, and therefore able to eat unsparingly without gaining an ounce. Pamela was envious. Ian ate little and looked dismal, distracting Pamela's mind and impeding her digestion as well.

The newlywed couple, proceeding hand in hand from one noisy table to the next in this huge room, accepted congratulations and kisses. They seemed placid, but smiles were mechanical. The father of the groom wiped his lips with a napkin before he got up and made an unholy show of bussing the bride. Ian, watching only briefly, looked sadder than ever. Pamela didn't entirely blame him. Kinnon, having noted the boy's mood yet again, decided that it was becoming unlikely that anything would galvanize him into a show of good feelings.

Ian declined to accept his portion of a tray of

creamy-looking cake. Pamela promptly gestured for the warm pastry to be put before the boy.

"You will regret not eating it when you see everyone else doing so."

Kinnon shook his head at her, indicating that she had picked the wrong way to deal with her brother. Pamela kept from pointing out that he himself had obtained no better results in what both recognized as an ongoing conflict to put the boy into better spirits. The dispute, to her surprise and most likely to Kinnon's, had become a testing ground for the effectiveness of his diplomatic maneuvering as against her desire for directly confronting any difficulty large or small.

As for Ian, who didn't particularly like such desserts, under his sister's eye he finished the glacé cake. He did not, however, contrive to smile afterward.

No clear victor had emerged between Pamela and Kinnon.

When supper was finished, the younger folk of Pamela's age were together. For a moment she wanted very much to join these strangers and overhear them making plans for a future about which they could know little if anything.

But there was a legend among females that many an engagement had been determined upon at the wedding of someone else in the same age group, and Pamela would have liked to guess which couples might be struck by the lightning on this occasion.

It amused her to see the bride's mother, an awesome-looking woman, in serious discussion with the fortunate Glenda. Beyond any doubt, the bride was being warned not to be a virtual doormat for her new husband or his family.

Kinnon, whose eyes met hers in shared amusement, looked down at Ian. A sigh had emanated from this source.

"I think we can make our departure now," he suggested.

He didn't have to concede that he was galled by the failure of his self-appointed mission to cheer up Pamela's brother. Nor was it necessary to add, she felt sure, that he would be transmitting a useful gift for the happy couple within the next week or so.

Making their adieux posed a difficulty. The fathers were occupied in a momentarily amiable discussion, causing Kinnon to hesitate before making an approach. Both men turned jovially to the peer, however, their breaths reeking of whiskey and strong wine.

The groom's mother had drawn the attention of her opposite number and both were talking loudly.

"Now it's a larger family with more troubles," said the latter.

"Yes, and it will be larger before you can snap two fingers." The groom's mother wanted to avoid a possible burst of sentimental tears from the in-law, or perhaps from herself. "Do you know that music hall song about the mums-in-law?"

"Oh yes." Glenda's mother experienced an instantaneous change of mood at being reminded of a song with lyrics that would apparently be pertinent to her feelings. She astonished everybody by moving her feet, right to left, left to right, as if in preliminary to a dance. Then her hands gripped the other's. The half-cracked and mostly drink-touched voice rumbled out some of the words in rhythm, a cockney accent imposed on them to fit the interpretation as heard in the halls:

" 'Oo does so much to 'elp a marriage?
'Oo offers so much common sense?"

The groom's mother grinned in response, moving her feet similarly. Husbands began to interfere, but held back as she had already begun singing the other part:

" 'Oo buys the 'osses and the carriage
With pounds and shillings and pence?"

Together the two women sang:

"The mums-in-law,
The mums-in-law.
They rub everybody else's nerves ruddy raw,
But they do their bleedin' best to 'elp a
marriage.
When yer temper is gone,
An' yer can 'ardly go on,
Yer can always depend on the mums-in-law.
(The owld cows!)
Yer can always depend on the mums-in-
law."

The two women held hands and danced together in a circle, laughing and singing till they could do no more of either.

Pamela was the first to look at Ian when an unaccustomed sound issued from his throat. The boy was chuckling. His lips were wide apart, his eyes gleamed. Recognizing the appearance of genuine pleasure from the much older pair, he had responded to it as cheerfully as everyone else in the gigantic room.

Kinnon glanced from the boy to Pamela. Her ready smile turned to coolness. Admittedly, the boy was behaving well at this time, but it wasn't to the peer's credit any more than to hers. Nonetheless, the peer was handsome, and though she didn't like him too well because of his indirect approach to others, she didn't feel it would be an act of torture to see him at some time in the near future.

CHAPTER 8
Unexpected Knowledge

The good feelings on all sides lasted, as far as Pamela was concerned, until the moment that Kinnon's carriage arrived before the comfortable house that Aunt Rosemary had rented for this month.

Kinnon departed from the vehicle first, then helped Pamela descend. Wisely, he left it to Ian to jump down.

"You had best go inside," Kinnon told the boy. "And instruct (I think her name is Charity) to do likewise."

Ian nodded, then drew out a hand to be clasped in a gingerly fashion, and spoke his thank you with sincerity but no mawkishness. Once those duties had been accomplished, he spoke more loudly to the maid.

"I must leave now, too," Pamela said, knowing full well that he wanted to keep her in place under the wheat-colored sliver of moon over their heads. "Several rooms are lighted, as you can see, and my aunt may be entertaining by herself."

"Of course, in a moment." He smiled winningly and came closer.

Pamela had to take three steps backward, feeling disappointed with fate and its curious workings.

"It is not that I don't want to be friendly," she began.

"Good. Everything is so much simpler when a young lady doesn't make small talk in which she suddenly invokes virtue and appearances along with other irrelevant matters."

"Nevertheless," she began, but didn't finish.

His right hand had touched the glove of her left. Pamela experienced an agreeable shock in each finger of the hand so honored.

The pressure grew against her and then his other hand circled her midriff. She would have sworn he hadn't moved forward far enough to reach her, but the deed was swiftly accomplished. Moving away was the work of a moment, and she turned her back to him.

"No, I will not," she said, feeling that ice was caught in her vocal chords despite the warm June air. "I am not indifferent to your presence, but too much lies between us for our relations to move further ahead, your lordship, I fear."

The Earl surely understood that determination of hers, practiced seducer that Kinnon must have been. Using force to get his way would make it impossible for each to see the other again. He stood unmoving, then stepped backward.

"My pardons, Miss Pamela," he said quietly.

At which words, Pamela told herself beyond doubt that she was going to be safer than she may have deserved.

There was a softening in her features of which Kinnon couldn't have been aware. It was an unusual man who could think in terms of a woman's emotions and feelings without displaying unease in word or deed. As a sop to his vanity, therefore, and without any other conceivable motive, she adopted a viewpoint that she told herself determinedly she didn't actually feel.

"I, too, am subject to various temptations, but I cannot indulge them at this time certainly," Pamela said. "Please take your leave now."

"Farewell," he said softly. "I will see you

again, and it may then be possible to move you further."

"Not by temporizing, by delaying, by indirectness, and by hoping that problems will solve themselves." Had she been so pointed in her speech, as if angry that he should have such a nature but willing to accept him otherwise? It seemed hardly possible. "Good night, your lordship."

"Good night, Miss Pamela," said a slightly dazed peer.

To leave some other impression with him beside one of bitter anger, she added, "I had forgotten to thank you for a pleasant afternoon and early evening."

Those words hovered in the cool air. They might just as well have remained unspoken. The peer was already making his way back to the carriage.

Pamela walked into the summer home and discovered that once again her life had changed for reasons entirely beyond her control.

"Certainly the time has come," Mr. Dickon Granbrook's familiar voice was saying.

The railroad *entrepreneur* was seated on the best chair in the large sitting room, legs wide apart. Perpetually red-faced and on the verge of issuing *fiats* or losing his temper entirely, he was of course dressed in formal black, with a white shirt and string tie. He was one of the builders of some new railway, and during the time of Aunt Rosemary's mourning, when he and his family had come to visit from Cumberland and been most helpful, he had often spoken about the problem of losing Sir John Conroy's influence and the glorious task of carrying supplies on the new network in case Europe became troublesome again. He had the curious facility of stepping into a drawing room, himself in full fig, and reminding witnesses of a presence in some barracks of the Army. An impression of raucous laughter seemed to follow him.

"My dear wife has seen to it that Dilys has learned what it is necessary for a young female to know about social matters, and it is time that Dilys was tested against the husband hunters of London itself. Now that schools for young ladies have done their worst, let us see how she adapts to real life in gaining the hand of a wealthy peer."

"Of course," Aunt Rosemary murmured, with a look of gratitude that Pamela had arrived.

"You are so right, dear," said Mr. Granbrook's wife. Olympia Granbrook was a tall woman with a look of patience that hadn't yet been refined to a look of martyrdom. "I can imagine dear Dilys being presented at court."

The daughter, in a sky-blue brocade grenadine with Spanish lace to show off her fair complexion, looked as if that observation had been made many times in her hearing.

Pamela, having greeted the elders respectfully and exchanged a hug with Dilys, found herself also visualizing the presentation at St. James's. Having been introduced through somebody already presented, the pallid girl would wear white flowers with a bodice in a round décolletage showing the shoulder and short sleeves, dark ostrich feathers and gloves. Her name would be read out by the Lord Chamberlain, whereupon Dilys would advance gratefully, curtsying very low as the Queen extended a hand to be kissed. Dilys would then rise and curtsy to such other members of the royal family as might have deigned to be present, carefully keeping her face to the Queen until she had left the presence chamber. . . .

Mr. Granbrook had apparently determined, perhaps belatedly, that a foot had to be put down if Dilys was ever to do him and his wife proud. No longer would Dilys be called "my baby" in the presence of physically suitable young males and be congratulated upon having beaux. This last was a habit of Mrs. Granbrook's. Dilys had still not recovered from feeling like an ugly infant on those first occasions, and remained so embarrassed that she had rarely been at ease in the presence of any of the first males who showed a courteous interest in her.

One time a young man had come to escort her to a ball, and her mother had said, with apparent pleasure, "She's all dressed up for tonight, but tomorrow she goes back to being my little baby."

Dilys had also told her friend from London about one particular young man with the ambition to enter the Commons. Her father, as a result, wouldn't permit Dilys to see him. In the meantime, however, she had discovered the thrill of being liked by a handsome man who sometimes blushed when she appeared in his orbit, a young man she could turn into jelly by a few words or a quiet smile.

This one wouldn't be put off. A meeting between him and the Granbrooks was inevitable. While Mrs. Granbrook spoke weakly about "my baby," in the same tone, probably, that Aunt Rosemary used when calling Pamela "child," Mr. Granbrook promptly forbade the house to the young man and forbade Dilys to see him ever again. Trying to discuss the matter was hopeless. The railroad builder had snobbishly determined that his daughter would marry none other than a peer of wealth. Unlike some members of the Commons or the Lords, for that matter, Mr. Dickon Granbrook's mind was not subject to being changed on any matter whatsoever.

Pamela and her friend looked at each other. Dilys allowed herself a long deep breath that couldn't possibly be interpreted by the imperceptive father as a sigh of resignation to the inevitable. Father persistently demanded she marry only a certain type of man, a keenly sought-after specimen of the breed and one who might not want to marry the daughter of a railroad builder from Cumberland. Mother tried to keep her like a child so that Dilys would probably not think of herself as having grown older. Indeed this was a two-horned dilemma!

"Therefore," Mr. Granbrook resumed, as if concluding a peroration that would justify a soul-wrenching decision, "I am bringing my daughter and wife to London."

"Another little visit from the three of you can do no harm whatever," Aunt Rosemary said.

Pamela was startled that the paterfamilias should feel the course of action to be so important. Further, it crossed her mind to ask herself what the Granbrook elders would say when they heard about Pamela's scandalous *défi* of constituted authority.

"A longer visit is planned," Mr. Granbrook explained. "Three months at least."

"Do you mean that you will all be in *le monde* while a suitable husband is sought for Dilys?"

"My wife and daughter will be in London for that time," Mr. Granbrook said a little rigidly. "I cannot spare so long a hiatus from my business affairs. I am therefore proceeding to ensconce them in a suitable hotel and will be leaving shortly afterward."

"I see," Pamela said, taken aback by the man's assurance that the major task would be accomplished in roughly ninety days.

"Three months should certainly be sufficient for a girl like my daughter," said Mr. Granbrook proudly.

Dilys looked down, not knowing whether to make some mock-modest remark. It didn't seem to have occurred to the proud father that many an attractive young woman was languishing in *le monde* for want of a suitable consort. Had the point been raised, Mr. Granbrook would have responded patronizingly that such difficulties could never apply to a girl as fetching as his Dilys. The railroad mogul may have been loud, overbearing, and arrogant, but his belief in the only descendant of his loins was nothing less than touching.

"You are right to expect no difficulty for dear Dilys," said Aunt Rosemary, exercising her great capacity for tactful comment.

The father acknowledged this home truth by a firm nod. "However, we do need aid from you and Pamela. Persons with *cachet,* as they call it, in society have to be available to introduce Dilys to the proper people."

"Of course," Aunt Rosemary conceded, and then her eyes opened wide in astonishment.

"You hadn't written to Mrs. Granbrook about how long you expect to stay out here," the father said as if he was referring by this last to some dim outpost of empire. "We assumed that you wouldn't want to absent yourself too long from the social season."

And he looked at Pamela as if to add that it wasn't everyone with a problem in marrying off a female relative.

Pamela turned to her aunt but spoke to the guest. "Perhaps you are unaware, sir—"

Aunt Rosemary interrupted. "Pamela, it is necessary to be of aid to our friends because they have been of aid to us."

Pamela refrained from asking how Aunt Rosemary expected a pariah to provide entrée into society for anyone else. No doubt she felt that her presence and Pamela's in hostile territory would be an earnest of good will. Nonetheless, it did seem that Kinnon's patience would be extended near the breaking point if she left Worthsea at this time. The peer would probably feel that her migration expressed complete disapproval. Lloyd Wilcoxen, the Earl of Kinnon, may not have been her favorite among mortals, as Pamela was careful to remind herself, but she was far from feeling the complete abhorrence with which their relationship had begun and only recently resumed. A change had taken place almost without her being aware of it.

Aunt Rosemary, determined to pay the debt

she had incurred to these Granbrooks one and all, drew herself to her full height.

"We leave tomorrow," she informed Pamela in a tone that would brook no denial, "and return to London."

CHAPTER 9
A Lovers' Meeting Before Journey's End

Dilys Granbrook dreaded meeting new people as a rule, and yet these nearly always liked her. Convinced that she had no skills, she was nonetheless able to play the piano, to sew and read and write German as well as a certain odious Corsican's adopted language of French. Arithmetic pleased her, and she occasionally did exercises of that nature, but only in secret.

Not every subject could be mastered with such unlikely ease. Mother had wanted her to take singing lessons, perhaps as a way of curing the very real shyness which often came upon her. A distinguished soprano had been hired for the purpose, and progress seemed gratifying until her voice broke one day on the barcarole from *Marino Faliero* and she refused to attempt singing for two full years. The piano had represented an uneasy compromise. Playing far more swiftly than the music demanded, she seemed to want to have her contacts with melody terminated as soon as might be. However, it was possible for her to begin and conclude a selection without wanting to fall dead afterward.

"It is a social accomplishment, my baby," Mother pointed out. "You cannot expect a young man to take serious interest in you on that far-off day when you are old enough to attract one, if you don't have social graces."

How was it possible to understand Mother? She said she looked forward to Dilys' marriage and purchased clothing of good quality to show her off; but always referred to her as "my baby." The words rankled, as if offering proof that many duties were performed mechanically and without conviction.

Looking at herself in the mirror on their first morning at Wimmer's Hotel on Bruton Street off Piccadilly, Dilys wished that her fresh young face showed more in it of worldly experience. Those last words were two that she had encountered in print, along with others on occasion. Mother, of course, took not the slightest notice of her child's good figure and features.

"Let us hope that the hair will grow out further," she said.

"I think I have grown quite well in other places," Dilys responded, looking down at her chest as seen in a good grade of Irish poplin.

Had the family not been in London to resolve the matter of her future, she would probably not have indulged herself in such daring.

"Gentlemen don't like bulges," Mother snapped as if she regretted having broached any part of the subject.

Impishly her daughter asked, "Are there any other things that gentlemen don't like?"

Mother promptly changed the subject. "At least your dress isn't dark gray, a color I could never abide! Now straighten up and don't suddenly sink into it! Turn and let your mother see how it has been cut to the hem. . . . Well, perhaps that should have been made just a trifle shorter. The way you often clump about, Dilys, you may trip over it. I shall ask Jennifer to take up the hem, and perhaps let it out just a little more at the chest because—"

Mother suddenly interrupted herself to stare, then sat down in the small but sparsely furnished chamber. She looked stunned.

"You will soon become a young woman, my baby. Not only will you walk out, you will marry and have children of your own. You will have to experience all the rituals, so to speak."

Although Mother had briefly made an important concession, to Dilys' way of thinking, it was impossible to be certain whether the premise of her conversation should be pursued any further. Nevertheless, it did seem that the iron was more than lukewarm. It was time to strike.

"Mother, what is a ritual?"

"A custom, my baby. For example, being escorted by a gentleman."

Dilys already knew about that particular ritual, having experienced it in Castlerigg. It held no mystery for her.

"What about the 'performance of wifely duties'? Is that a ritual, too?"

That was another phrase she had encountered in print, in *The Woman's Paper*, a copy of which was kept on Mother's sewing table at home. It seemed that at the beginning of her first full day on this mission to capture a husband of wealth and position, she ought to be told about what being a wife entailed.

"You shouldn't speak of that." Mother closed her eyes as if in horror of something she couldn't bear to contemplate. "When the time comes, not just yet, it will be clear to you as it was clear to me. You may rest assured of that much."

No more information was vouchsafed on that subject, although Mother was willing to speak about social happenings in those early married years with Father.

None of Dilys' friends back home in Castlerigg had been able to offer any help in clearing up that question, either. One of them had thought it somehow involved Lord Melbourne, the Queen's First Minister.

Because of the change of venue to this First City of the World, Dilys determined upon putting that query to Father. Years had passed since she used to shake at the knees whenever she found herself in his overpowering presence. At the very least, Dilys hoped, Mr. Granbrook would direct Mother to proffer the knowledge that their daughter was now seeking.

Mr. Dickon Granbrook was soon discovered in a corner of the so-called parlor room of the family's suite in the Hotel Wimmer. He was rarely at his sunniest in the best of times, but now his mood was low indeed. Business may have been satisfactorily done after consultations with bankers, but in London he felt like one more man of business among a plethora of duplicates. At Castlerigg he felt like the most majestic presence in all of Cumberland. Small wonder he didn't relish visits to the great metropolis!

Dilys, herself so delighted at the burgeoning of extensive contact with a great world beyond Cumberland, found him scowling at a newspaper.

"Father, what are—?" Too late she realized that she had embarked on a lunatic endeavor but felt she had already carried it too far to pull back. "Mother has told me a little, but perhaps you can inform me about everything else."

"Well, speak out, girl!" He looked less favorably disposed than before, his legs only inches apart on an ottoman that was several sizes too small for his preference. "Ask me what you want to know and do it this instant!"

"I—I wish to be told what is meant by the words 'wifely duties.' "

A breath, drawn in deeply by someone else, caused Dilys to look around. Mother had entered and, of course, overheard the request.

"Your daughter is far too young to be told about such matters," Mother said starchily. "It should also be pointed out to her that certain matters are simply not raised by children when in mixed company."

"She is on the point of marriage," said Father portentously and, Dilys hoped, correctly. "It wouldn't be fair or right to ignore the request."

"Mr. Granbrook!" Mother was scandalized.

Dilys said quickly, "I beg your pardon, Pappa, and Mamma's as well, if I have overstepped any bounds." Politeness from a parent, or anyone else, demanded a suitable return.

"The problem won't go away because of a sudden onset of good manners," Father said with a probing look.

Dilys was aware of shaking at the knees in his presence for the first time since early childhood.

"I am sure that before you marry, daughter, your mother will explain as much to you as it will be suitable for you to know beforehand."

There was a look between the elders, as if sharing a secret. Mother looked away first.

"For the moment, it ought to be sufficient if I avoid the sort of excesses, the leering, that one sees in certain so-called newspapers that are published in this city, and—"

Mother emitted a protest at the very conception of leering, no doubt, whatever that might have been. Dilys made a mental note to inquire about those leering newspapers. Pamela, who would be joining her in a little while, was certain to know of them.

"For the moment," Mr. Granbrook continued, "it ought to be sufficient if I say that the words 'wifely duties' don't refer only to making sure that a house is well run in every way."

Dilys palpably wanted further clarification. She looked mulishly unprepared to budge if it wasn't offered.

"What is referred to, Dilys, is something more personal, more intimate."

Now Dilys felt a flush mounting hotly to her cheeks.

"I ought to tell you that there are women who claim that they cannot endure wifely duties, which may be true." His eyes left hers, and Dilys didn't want to know where they had briefly alighted. "Other women truly loathe wifely duties. Still others are neutral to them. The most fortunate ones among married womanhood—"

Once more some sounds issued from between Mother's lips. On the point of rebuking Father once again, she had apparently changed her mind.

"It is best to enjoy these matters, these wifely duties," Mr. Granbrook proceeded, "even to relish them if at all possible. The woman who feels that way is happy. Now do you understand?"

Dilys shook her head. No information had really been transmitted.

"You will understand more fully in time." Father's voice was raised now. Loud and commanding, it was a dismissal after having offered nothing but tantalizing indications. Perhaps he felt that enough of his valuable time had been occupied. Sulkily he returned to his newspaper, which was probably far from the leering sort to which he had contemptuously and mysteriously referred.

Mother agreed with alacrity to let Dilys wait downstairs in the lobby of the Wimmer for Pamela Forrest to arrive and take her for a carriage ride about the great city. No doubt Mrs. Granbrook was happy to be relieved if only for a while of the presence of a daughter who raised troublesome questions. Dilys, in her turn, wanted to think undisturbed about the information that had just been passed on, which amounted to very little in her view at the moment.

There was a comfortable satinwood chair in the large lobby, and it faced an opened square window with a view of Bruton Street in June. The Wimmer catered to families of some position and to farmers who could afford brief jousts with residents of the City.

Dilys stretched out, an unusual deed for a young girl of good social position in an almost public place. There wasn't much unsupervised leisure allotted to her and doing what she wanted in midmorning was a great luxury.

On a nearby duo-chair, speaking softly, were a well-dressed young man and a female in striped silk with shirred ruffles. The dress boasted a wire framework that made it bulge out so that from the neck down she almost resembled a show horse in some tableau. Mistakenly, Dilys assumed it was part of a current London style.

"But if we're found out!" the girl said in alarm, causing Dilys to listen intently. Her voice was muffled by a raised newspaper held between her left profile and the outer world.

"Oh, use your loaf, girl!" the man snapped, controlling himself in a tone that Mr. Granbrook's daughter wasn't the only female to have encountered. "We won't be found out, and this will do you good."

"Marriage would do me even more good," the girl insisted.

Dilys sat up, being careful not to make a sound. All she had to do was put down her feet noisily or to cough and both miscreants would run off or change the subject.

"Now, luv, you know that maybe in time I'll marry you as soon as I feel it's possible."

"How *I* feel is that we ought to marry, and quick!"

The gentleman indicated that the subject of her feelings on this one subject didn't currently absorb him.

"You don't really care about me! You just want me as a wife without portfolio, a wife without your having to marry me."

It seemed to the listener that she was coming close to the heart of that mystery at home, the mystery of intimate matters. She wished her lips hadn't become so dry and feared that her heart's hammering must alert the others before she knew more about *it*, whatever it was.

The girl miscreant must have heard some remark that wasn't clear to Dilys because her change of mood was as quick as summer lightning.

"That's *impossible!*"

"I've done it before, my girl, and I can do it again. 'Strewth!"

A hornet buzz of sound came from the girl. Dilys listened in vain, fists clenched, hands crossed and held tightly to her, hoping silently that she would learn more about this mystery which she felt instinctively was part of the other one.

"We'll go upstairs now," the man said. "And I wish you'd get rid of that miserable newspaper! People will think that we're being underhanded in some way."

The girl lowered it. Her face was customarily pale, but vexation had brought red spots to her cheeks. Unable to find a location for the paper, she eased it to the carpeted floor and stood up to follow the impatient young man.

Moving cautiously after having followed the miscreants with her eyes, Dilys stood up. Promises to herself tumbled over one another: never would she speak about this to anybody, never would she put herself into a situation such as that girl had done.

But it did seem to Dilys that a female of that type could have been occupied with reading matter that was likely to shed further illumination on the absorbing problem that confronted her restless intelligence.

With only a minimum of further ado, Dilys raised the penny sheet so that it would hide her features from the unwelcome scrutiny of any passerby inside the premises or without. *Society Favors*, which was the title of this misbegotten instance of journalism, gave no space to such otherwise newsworthy items as the Queen's difficulties with her Cabinet or the Parliament. Space was given to a description of a free-floating balloon that had apparently landed in Nassau, wherever that might be, but started out from Vauxhall. There was an account of the wedding of Maria II of Portugal to Ferdinand of Saxe-Coburg, but only prolonged reading would have made it clear that the event had taken place several years ago.

This penny sheet apparently dealt, in the main, with the doings of Londoners favored by wealth. No scandal among the poor was reported in these precincts, as far as Dilys could tell.

Nor was any information offered that would help to solve the problem she had set for herself. Angered by a diet of gammon-and-spinach, Dilys suddenly found her eyes opening wide and any thought of marital duties promptly forgotten almost as if it had never been.

A most familiar name was mentioned in this penny sheet. A set of circumstances involving the owner of that name was outlined forcefully. There was time to understand why her own attempts to snare a husband of wealth and position might come to nought.

Dilys ignored the opportunity to read about cricket scores, although it seemed that a match between Cumberland and Sussex teams had turned out favorably for one side. Glancing from left to right in order to be assured that no one was keeping watch upon her doings, she set the paper down on the carpeted floor and a distance away from this satinwood chair. Her hands shook as she did so, and she felt as if she had committed a theft.

Straightening herself quickly, she was in time to see a certain canoe landau, the property of Pamela's aunt, approach the curb. A notably difficult afternoon was beckoning to Dilys and her friend, the latter being the only occupant of the precinct within that vehicle. Dilys rose with all the dignity of a French aristocrat on the way to the nearest tumbrel.

CHAPTER 10
From a View to a Disturbance

Pamela would occasionally give some thought to the first governess who had ever been hired by Aunt Rosemary and Uncle Vincent to offer instruction to the youthful barbarian Pamela Forrest. The poor woman had been instructed to notify Aunt Rosemary if any difficulty whatever arose for Pamela. The child was delicate, Aunt Rosemary had insisted, whatever that meant. Pamela could recall that she liked being called delicate. It sounded important.

Further, Aunt Rosemary made the governess promise solemnly to bring Pamela to see her every two hours if she was at home. For months Aunt Rosemary had made a point of being at home all day. Pamela was embarrassed, she could recall, into feeling entirely helpless.

The recollection had come unbidden to her because of the attitude that Dilys was exhibiting. Shy at the best of times, she was now sitting almost as if she had rolled herself into a ball. Not even the German-English of Hope, the vacant-faced maid *("Zu Befehl,* miss"), had amused her. Hope, riding with the Forrest coachman, was another who probably felt insecure.

Seeing her friend's misery, Pamela had determined upon instructing the coachman to take both girls for a ride around the city. It would give them the opportunity to talk. Pamela intended to explain why she had been cast out of Eden and to add that she would do again what she had previously done. The explanation might not be popular, but it did seem that only in adversity did one identify friends.

Dilys, her mind on the difficulty which she faced as a result of Pamela's transgression, knew that she was being a bad friend by thinking of herself alone. The temptation, however, was wholly beyond her powers to resist.

"What is to be done now?" she asked after the carriage began to move and Hope uttered a prayerful wail intended for the ears of her Teutonic ancestors.

"The season is soon concluded, but there will be occasions where one can appear. There are sporting events, certainly. Horse racing, for example. Ascot is over by this time and Epsom Downs is not as exclusive as one would like.

There remains 'cup day' at Goodwood, in the wilds of Sussex. The ducal meeting should be useful for your purposes, and mine, though I hesitate to admit as much at the moment. I may add that I doubt whether Doncaster or Liverpool or Newmarket will be useful *pour le sport* as far as we are concerned."

Dilys asked sadly, "But would you be invited to mingle with the London Fashionables after what has happened?"

Pamela accepted the inevitable. News of her downfall had apparently been communicated to this visitor from Cumberland. Dilys, knowing the worst and being more of a good friend than she imagined, didn't scorn Pamela's company.

"I fear that I would not even be allowed into Tattersall's on the Monday following the race in order to settle my inevitable losing wager."

"Then *what* is to be done?"

The carriage had eased away from a smoother route and into the Little Ireland section. Under the weight of Hope's tearful requests and Teutonic profanations, the carriage left the rutted streets. Hope sounded little soothed by the Plough Road area, either, and seemed not at all taken by a caravansary called the Bells and Motley. From the carriage seats it sounded as though the maid was speaking and expectorating at the same time, which caricaturists often indicated was the nature of all speech apart from the purest English as spoken at Windsor by the Queen and her German Prince Consort.

"Our maid speaks in umlauts," Pamela said, smiling.

"Please excuse me if I am not convulsed," Dilys responded mildly enough. "I feel much the same as she does, if not for the same reasons."

"There is no need in either case, Dilys. Steps are under way to reclaim my shattered reputation."

The promise caused Pamela to recollect Kinnon's interest in what seemed like a project that might involve dredging if worse came to worst. She had written to him at the Albany about her sudden change of address, but no reply from him had yet been forthcoming.

"And until your situation is altered, I am helpless," her friend said in summary.

"I would not say that." Pamela smiled more lightly. "Further clarification will be given to you in good time."

The carriage left Prospect Row in Southwark and meandered along Townsend Street. Pamela took advantage of the excursion to tell Dilys why she had accomplished the feat of becoming *persona non grata* to the older members of good society. Dilys at least paid the tribute of listening silently, of making every effort to understand, of not interrupting with a crisp observation here or a muffled gibe at some other point. She was indeed a thoughtful friend, Pamela decided, not for the first time.

At the conclusion of a narrative which might have held Scheherazade herself in thrall, Pamela looked out at the position of the sun. It was no longer rising. She leaned forward and spoke to the driver.

"And now to our muttons, such as they might be," Pamela said. "As you shall discover almost momentarily, dear sister, there is a balm in Gilead."

The landau changed direction, disconcerting a street sweeper, who nearly struck his midriff against one of the hitching posts. Deftly, an omnibus was avoided, but the driver of a battered dray cursed the Forrest coachman and any descendants he might beget. Ill-dressed children ran in front of the carriage horses and performed cartwheels, only to be rewarded with stray coppers from amused onlookers.

"Where are we going?" Dilys asked, having kept from calling out with the sort of dismay that Hope had once again clearly demonstrated from her perch.

"Once you see what I have in mind, no explanations will be needed."

Little enough time lurched past before Dilys did indeed understand what point her friend had been attempting to make. Miss Granbrook's first thought was in the form of questioning if the vaunted march of civilization could have brought humankind to the situation which confronted her widened if not entirely incredulous eyes.

By dint of driving the horses along the Bayswater Road, the two girls had reached that precinct of Hyde Park which was called the Ladies' Mile. At almost four o'clock of this June afternoon, men and women could be seen on horseback reconnaissance, inspecting each other as they rode about slowly. Some of the females were accompanied by chaperones of various types. Some men were on foot. All of the participants looked like different breeds of waterfowl that had ventured away from the protection offered by the Serpentine.

"Is this where you take me to find a—" The

word "suitor" was trembling on Dilys' lips, but she couldn't speak it.

"You must not be shy, dear sister." Pamela smiled, having either misunderstood or understood too well the nature of her friend's response. With a gloved hand she smoothed the russet crinoline and used her other gloved palm to gentle down one of the ruffled tulle sleeves of the garment. Keenly she looked out. Sunlight, she decided once more, had the effect of brightening her red hair even further than must have been originally intended. "All may yet be well."

"But this is almost a vegetable market!"

Pamela winced at language that seemed unnecessarily precise. Loath to admit it though she may have been, it had crossed her mind that the Earl of Kinnon might be discovered prowling in the area. With Kinnon's reputation firmly in mind, Pamela had wanted to show that she, too, could take some role in *la vie sportif* should she choose. Circumstances had caused her to arrive in the company of this good friend from an outlying area.

"Many London Fashionables come to meet here," she remarked, having decided at last that Kinnon was not among those at this afternoon's *dansant* without music.

"Fashionables are not always wealthy, from what I am given to understand." Dilys was recollecting bulletins that had been remorsefully issued by belles back at Castlerigg, sorrowful young ladies communicating delphically after long consultations with parents and governesses and, in some cases, surgeons.

"My dear pappa," Dilys began, and wondered if she wasn't being unreasonable in referring to one of those ornaments of social life of which Pamela was wholly bereft, "will not, as you know, consent to my marriage with anyone but a titled man of wealth."

"There are some males nearby who conform to that description."

"But no ladies. Not that one, for example."

Dilys had briefly pointed toward a young female seated sidesaddle on a tired horse. Some of her straw hair seemed strategically loosened as she leaned forward to speak with a tall young man on foot. Dilys noticed, too, that the female's hands were folded behind her back, giving an aura of romantic surrender in public.

"That woman," said Pamela, her voice rising, "is Lady Suzanne Boyce. I have in the past years considered her a friend of mine, but not in adversity of any sort."

Lady Suzanne turned, having heard herself referred to with words that were well on this side of idolatry. She smiled thinly, and raised her voice too.

"How good to see you once again, Miss Forrest," she said carefully. "I had no thought that you would show yourself in public so soon after having been disgraced by your own actions."

Pamela leaned forward to make her voice carry a little further. "I am not mortified to know *everyone* who comes to Rotton Row."

"And you have brought a friend, I see," Lady Suzanne proceeded, shifting the focus of her attentions. "Someone I don't recognize at all and who must know very little about you."

In the course of these interchanges the young man to whom Lady Suzanne had been speaking was entirely ignored. His eyes caught sight of the lovely Miss Granbrook, features flushed. His jaw dropped. It seemed as if he had heard about beautiful young women but had never actually encountered one of the species until this moment.

Approaching the carriage courteously on the way to Pamela's side, he seemed unable to prevent himself from continuing his close examination of Miss Granbrook. Dilys, who had been looked at with awe by other young men sternly forbidden by Mr. Granbrook to know her, took advantage of this burst of freedom to stare back at him.

The young man who faced her was clean-shaven and with rather fine features for an exemplar of the opposite sex. He seemed tall. Perceptively Dilys supposed that the height had presented something of a drawback to such social aspirations as were his.

"How do you do?" he said, almost as if he was on the point of choking. A deep breath offered some small relief, but he was unable to prevent himself from gasping. "Miss, I am honored."

Pamela said quickly, "This gentleman is Avery Holt. He, like his father, is a solicitor."

Without using the words directly, she couldn't have made it more clear that Avery lacked a title. Certainly he earned an income, but not of the magnitude to satisfy an empire-builder like Dickon Granbrook, Pamela felt certain.

His manners won approval from Mr. Granbrook's issue, however, as might have been expected. Dilys was nonetheless unable to avoid the conclusion that he was attempting to redress the balance over any injury that Lady Suzanne

Boyce might have perpetrated. As a result, she merely inclined her head. It would have been difficult, because of her own shyness, to speak with him. No words presented themselves easily to facilitate discussion with someone who apparently thought of her as a deity come to earth.

She turned to her friend. "Are we leaving shortly?"

Pamela nodded, then looked away. "Avery, I am sorry that your addresses cannot be welcomed in this instance."

"I—I must speak to—" He had halted.

An inspiration now came to Avery Holt. He was not a young man revered across the length and breadth of the Empire for the quality of his imagination, as has been seen, but he could occasionally rally such forces as he possessed.

"I must speak to you, Pamela. I have heard from the Earl of Kinnon, and he mentioned your name."

The pages of this chronicle, in common with those of all recorded history, teem with instances of temptations met and overcome. Confronted by opportunities for profit of some sort as a result of the Devil's work, knights as well as varlets and ladies fair have held back and occasionally offered lengthy perorations to justify the noble actions. Upon this occasion, however, as a scrivener who is anxious to please must regretfully state, Miss Forrest gave in immediately.

Even as she paused, attentive, she was keenly aware of the dilemma that had been presented. It was in the best interests of Dilys and of Avery himself for both young ladies to depart posthaste. And yet the one name had been mentioned that must perforce result in Pamela's being chained to the spot if necessary until fresh information had been communicated.

Dilys, having observed the play of emotions upon her friend's features, sacrificed her own interests without a moment's thought.

"You must hear what Mr. Holt has to say, Pammie," she insisted. Nothing loath to remain, she was happy to witness Pamela's interest in the man her late uncle had wanted her to wed.

Pamela nodded. The landau remained in place.

Avery Holt accomplished the feat of speaking to Pamela while he looked over at Miss Granbrook.

"I encountered—ah, yes, Kinnon—earlier today," Avery proceeded. "He told me that he had gone to visit you at Worthsea but that you and your aunt had departed."

"Yes?"

The young solicitor's words tapered off. His body, perhaps because Dilys Granbrook had nodded encouragingly, took on the aspect of some trophy newly stuffed if not yet mounted on a hunter's wall.

"Kinnon said—oh, hang it! He said *something* else, I know he did."

"Very well, then. What was it?"

"I cannot seem to recollect it, although his statement is most assuredly part of the *res gestae*. The words will not come to me at this moment."

Dilys, showing great presence of mind, turned away. Without those unforgettable features to gaze at, Avery's senses became once more occupied with the presentation of facts.

"Kinnon told me that he hopes to see you on this night."

"Indeed. Perhaps I will be notified by him about the plans he has made in which I am included."

"He has written a note to you, which may have reached Clifford Street too late."

Pamela nodded, wondering if she had shown

elation. It would have been beyond her capacities to tell anyone how she felt about the Earl, wanting to see him again while detesting what seemed his well-honed ability at tergiversation. In an ideally constructed world, she would have found romance with Kinnon but marital respectability with someone whose mentality was far more congenial.

Avery's look had shifted from her features, and Pamela knew immediately that Dilys had turned back to him.

"No doubt a more full introduction is required," Pamela said, not wanting to add that the press of parental influence from her friend's side would make it wholly unnecessary. "Mr. Holt, you know of Dilys. Avery, this is Miss Granbrook, whose father"—a downward twist of her lips was Pamela's only display of sympathy for her friend—"is a great example to us all of the British Empire at its most venturesome."

"Mr. Granbrook?" Avery, his eyes never leaving Dilys' face, sounded puzzled. "I must be so unsettled I cannot recollect the name."

"Mr. Granbrook, Mr. Dickon Granbrook, has fully earned the right to demand that his daughter be allied only with the finest and most influential of Britain's sons. His incomparable service to the Empire has consisted of arranging for the construction of that great railroad from Castlerigg to Buttermere in Cumberland. During a recent visit he never wearied of speaking about the charms of this contrivance. Someone traveling to Buttermere by train is also able to return to Castlerigg by train. I might add that, as an unparalleled feat of engineering, the railroad actually spans the width of Buttermere Lake."

"I see." Avery almost certainly did understand that Dilys' father was a man puffed up by good fortune and fully prepared to put obstacles in the way of a suitor without a royal bloodline, at the very least. "Difficulties of any sort can be met with persistence."

Dilys flushed to the roots of her dark hair and looked down briefly. Pamela had been unprepared to see such ardor from a longtime friend such as Avery, although it was mercifully directed at another.

As he became silent, gazing his fill at the divinity in the far end of the carriage, it fell to Dilys to suggest indirectly that some progress be made in furthering the acquaintance.

"My feet are almost numb as a result of sitting in this carriage for such a long time," she said, demonstrating a talent for probable mendacity that Pamela had not previously noted in her.

It was Avery's turn to exhibit shyness on a level with that of his lady fair.

"I am very tall," he said in a voice more subdued than before.

Dilys was already leaving the carriage, forcing Pamela to turn her body to the left and plant both limbs closer to the seat. Dilys emerged at last, having been hesitantly aided by Mr. Holt.

"There is indeed a distance to look up at you," she smiled. "In the future, however, I could purchase shoes that will give me a somewhat greater height."

"Why, yes, so you can!" Avery looked astonished at a solution of such awesome simplicity, one that had never occurred to him and would have been scorned by many a young lady of his acquaintance.

Pamela was infernally vexed by the mutual awed silence of these two. "May I suggest that both of you take out for a stroll?"

"Yes, I—of course." Avery had been unable to think so clearly as to make a suggestion.

"And I sincerely hope that the two of you will stay in my sight all the time, or I shall have to hunt you both down in my most ruthless fashion and with many a view halloo."

"Certainly," Avery Holt agreed, "if Miss Granbrook would care to—" He was unable to clarify a point that couldn't have been excessively obscure.

"I accept with the greatest—" Dilys began. The inability to complete a sentence was apparently contagious, for her voice trailed off into a tremulous breathing.

Pamela was left to conjecture what form a discussion would take between a male and a female so impressed by each other as to be unable to speak a thought in its entirety.

All in all, she would have infinitely preferred the company of Lloyd Wilcoxen, the Earl of Kinnon. Underhanded and dilatory he might be, but it was possible to express anger or irritation to him as well as rare good feeling, and the additional freedom was worth its weight in one of those ridiculous-looking railroad trains.

CHAPTER 11
Another Labor for Hercules

Kinnon would be calling for her at nine o'clock, according to the note which he had inscribed in a firm and clear hand. The screed awaited her in her bedroom and she examined it before changing for supper. She felt grateful, among other blessings, that it had eventually been possible to pry Dilys away from Avery's company and convoy her back to the hotel at which she and her parents were staying. No doubt the Granbrooks would soon be apprised of Pamela's social *faux pas*, causing the paterfamilias to seek aid among such friends in business as he had accumulated by his railroad building.

After careful consideration, Pamela scorned the services of Charity and dressed herself. A lilac taffeta with open sleeves would show off the red hair. An *emperatrice* double scarf descending to the midriff would serve nicely for the outdoors, in case a carriage ride was to be attempted. A cap-crown and bonnet that was snow white where it was untouched by flower patterns would be suitable.

Supper on this night, with newly laid darkish red wallpaper in the room and a cozy warmth emanating from the very walls despite wide-opened windows, was a difficult meal from the start. Pamela, in high spirits, smilingly retailed the latest information about Kinnon's expected arrival.

Ian promptly demanded to know where the three of them would be going on this occasion, thereby causing a contretemps between himself and Pamela.

Aunt Rosemary rapped a butter knife against one of the dropsical water glasses. Heads were lowered and grace spoken in a steady voice. Aunt Rosemary kept one eye on the service that followed and the other upon her small family.

Ian ate lightly, no more than half a dozen tablespoons of the oyster soup and only a few slivers of the *capons à l'escarlate* in the remove. Aunt Rosemary ate generously of the roasted peacock and the pudding with its mutton and tongue, its chicken and egg and fruit spice. Pamela, her midriff aflutter, confined herself to the vanilla soufflé and Darjeeling tea that followed.

Ian suddenly said, "Ask the Earl and see if I can't go with him."

The temperature became higher in the room than heat itself would have warranted. Aunt Rosemary, her mind recalled from the golden past to the leaden present, clapped her hands once in disapproval.

"You have given sufficient annoyance," she said briskly. "Proceed to your room and think about your shortcomings."

Ian's walk upstairs, although made in the company of the family bulldog, Gaiter, was a slow one. He seemed certain that no one truly understood his feelings. The night was going to be a bleak one for him, in which neither the dog nor his lory bird would understand his feelings.

Pamela waited until her brother was out of earshot. "Children, I think, want everything to happen on the instant."

"And if a child is thwarted, he or she sees life as dismal and himself as the toad beneath the harrow," Aunt Rosemary said perceptively. "Only a well-fed youth can dream of himself or herself as a failure."

"It is proof that you have been a good surrogate mother to him," Pamela said thoughtfully, reminding herself that the same lesson applied as well to Ian Forrest's sister.

As she had anticipated, Aunt Rosemary accepted that homage with an amused nod and then a rueful shrug.

"Ah, well, the small frog always sees a forbidding pond."

It was an apothegm that Pamela had occasionally heard from Uncle Vincent. For his widow to speak it without attribution was confirmation of her growing acceptance of fate's intrusions.

Pamela drew out a hand toward the older woman as a symbol of friendship rather than the customary respect or fealty. It was accepted in complete understanding. . . .

At this juncture Hope, the downstairs maid, appeared unexpectedly in the dining room.

Aunt Rosemary, her lips thinned by momentary irritation held in check, asked, "Might I know the reason for this interruption?"

"*Jawohl*, mum," said the menial, mindful of her instructions to spice up her normal cockney with a dash of inherited Germanic flavor. "There is a visitor."

Pamela's heart was hammering furiously

against unexpectedly fragile ribs. Putting both hands on the table, she pushed her chair back.

Aunt Rosemary instructed gravely, "Bring him into the large sitting room, Hope."

Pamela waited, unmoving. When her aunt nodded at last, she hurried to the door and gripped the knob firmly before flinging it open. No one was in sight. The hallway boasted only of furnishings which had accumulated over many years and been shined by willing hands.

Kinnon was indeed to be found in the large sitting room. Calm and sure of himself, the head tilted, the body stance prepared for friendship or battle, he was on the premises again. Didn't the visit prove that hope remained for her?

"Miss Pamela!" The light gray eyes gleamed with pleasure. He took a step toward her, hands outstretched. Reminded by her astonishment at the position he actually occupied in her life, his lordship drew back. "As you see, I am here. I received your recent missive and can only assume in turn that you received mine."

"Yes, but I am not certain that I can accede to your request for an evening in your company." She felt tempted, often, to say something inflammatory to this agreeable peer.

Wasn't it possible that she might otherwise speak words which she would regret even more keenly?

"Might I ask what the difficulty is?"

"I am not aware of being able to go any place tonight where we would both be seen together."

He was startled. "Excuse me?"

"It was agreed that we would want to be observed in each other's society and presumably considering the prospect of obeying the wishes of my late uncle and your late father." It was annoying almost beyond reason that so vital a consideration should have fled the precincts of his intelligence.

"Oh yes, of course."

"But I don't know of any significant gathering that will take place tonight at which we could make such an impression," she added. "No attendance at a gambling house or theater would be of use in achieving that goal."

"Conceded."

"In that case, I see no reason to consider the matter at this time."

She had expected some quick protest and an avowal of feeling for her. A reminder of the kiss they had shared in Worthsea, a lingering kiss in

Pamela's recollection, would not have been ill received.

His agreement in silence took her entirely unaware. She must have looked as unsettled as she felt. Annoyance showed in her features because he had undoubtedly observed it.

"Very well," she said slowly, making an apology for her attitude without speaking such words. She tilted her head up, signifying that her pride remained untouched. "Please tell me how you plan to meet the situation."

"As I have indicated, I do not have a plan to confront that particular difficulty tonight," he said. "Another issue, however, remains to be settled."

"I am not aware of it."

"You should be," he said quickly, and then smiled by way of offering his own unspoken apology. He was a surprisingly proud man, it seemed, demonstrating at least one trait of character that she thoroughly approved. "I refer to your certainty that I am weak and temporizing by nature. It follows that I cannot therefore make my wishes felt, in your opinion, or be of the least use in effecting change of any sort."

"Would you attempt to prove otherwise?" If she tilted her head up any higher, she would receive a bothersome series of twinges in the back of the neck.

"I would and will." His smile was ready. "In your presence, of course."

At least one facile insult sprang to her lips immediately, but she left it unspoken. He had earned a chance to prove his point, and she was realizing how much she wanted to accept his evaluation of himself.

"I assume that a chaperone will be desired," she said, and his sudden flush was accompanied by hers. "We will utilize the services of Charity, then, as Hope remains unsettled after the last revel."

"I can but hope that Charity is more phlegmatic by nature," the Earl observed.

"She is a realist, so to say." Pamela blinked. "Might I ask what herculean labor you are proposing to equal by your exploit on this night?"

He took the question seriously. "I think that it is about time the Augean stables were cleaned, Miss Pamela. In part, at the very least."

"It sounds as if the night's activities will be novel ones for a gently nurtured female."

He apparently halted himself from bowing in acknowledgment. There was a smile on his lips and he briefly drew a closed hand upward to cover them.

"On that point, Pamela," he said, for once eschewing the honorific, "I can firmly assure you. It is very likely that you will find the next hours unforgettable in the extreme."

CHAPTER 12
A Kiss After the Battle

At this point in the narrative, the chronicler confesses to feelings of vexation. Quill in hand, foolscap at the ready, a freshet of words available from the recesses of capacious memory, it nonetheless becomes a matter of imposing difficulty to attempt a description of the feelings of Pamela Forrest at this time.

We have dwelt sufficiently, perhaps, upon her confused responses to the courtship of a man unlike any she would have preferred to admire and come to love. Her feelings upon being made an heiress and refusing the bounty as offered have been expatiated upon. It would seem that whatever could be indited about Miss Forrest has already found its way to the proliferation of sheets that lie before the assiduous chronicler. This, however, is not so.

An entirely new stimulus was now to appear in her life, bringing forth responses unlike any that she had previously experienced.

The carriage ride began inauspiciously, with

Charity beside the coachman rather than the belowstairs *Gräfin*, Hope. Kinnon kept a respectful distance from Pamela, smiled frequently, and offered courteous remarks about the weather (warm and fine, quite unlike London's usual), the political situation (Bobby Peel would certainly become the First Minister to the Queen), and other matters of no importance whatever in Pamela's current view. About their destination, however, he said nothing.

It soon became evident that the carriage was leaving London. Pamela, with the stirring of concern, looked out to one side.

"Fear not," said his lordship affably, admiring her profile. "You will be safer tonight than some of the people you are going to see."

This ambiguous remark was sufficient to cause Pamela to consider demanding an explanation and leaving the carriage if none was offered. The conception soon occurred to her that Kinnon was preparing her thus for one or more encounters of a type never dreamt of in her philosophy, to quote the words of a well-known playwright. Rarely in life had she been more restive.

"We are in Surrey," his lordship said as she strained to discern the print upon a signpost that passed too quickly, as it happened. "In Lingfield, specifically."

She did not immediately identify Blindley Heath when the carriage halted. One reason for her deficiency was that she had rarely been here after nightfall. Another, to be sure, was simply that she had never in her life seen the heath or any other place in such a turmoil.

To be sure, the humans who were present accounted for the aforesaid turmoil rather than the heath itself. It seemed that several men were holding torches aloft, much like hautboys in the City. By this illumination it was possible to perceive the appalling sight that presented itself.

There was a four-sided square under these lights, the sides marked by rope laid out diagonally and tied to posts. Within this impromptu not-quite-square were three men. One stood off to a side, alert and prepared to move forward in case he detected some need to do so.

The others were stripped to the waist and wore what looked like drawers that descended to a point just above the kneecaps. Each faced the other and was in motion, fists bare and extended in as ungainly a manner as a well-brought-up and now deeply shocked young lady might have imagined.

"Is this a—a fight for money?"

"Certainly," said his lordship. "The gladiator to our left is Arthur Burke, the Knave of Knightsbridge. A low fighter, he is capable of various effronteries to the hallowed name of good sportsmanship."

Before she could look away, the Knave had closed with his opponent, causing the other's knees to buckle. A spurt of blood was falling from the latter's right cheek.

"That other is named Ernest Osset, and his sobriquet will surprise you not at all after what you have just seen. He is known as the Bermondsey Bleeder. Anyone he contends with, no matter how inexperienced, will at some time draw claret. Ernest is justly celebrated for his capacity to take punishment."

"But this is illegal!" she protested. "I have read veiled accounts of such horrors and I know that the law imposes heavy penalties against whoever participates in the staging and even the witnessing of such contests."

"A few pence in the correct pockets," the Earl pointed out, "and perceptions are altered in regard to what is permissible and legal."

Pamela closed her eyes at the sound of a sudden shout from the audience. Beyond question, Bermondsey had once more demonstrated his peculiar gift.

"How long will it last?"

"This round is going to be over in time," Kinnon said. "The lengths of the various rounds, as each individual joust is called, tend to vary. The rest periods between rounds vary as well. The time used depends upon the abilities of certain takers of wagers to elicit sufficient sums, whereupon they signal for rounds to be continued or commence or be halted, as the case may be."

"How long does this entire event last?" Her eyes remained stubbornly closed.

"Until one contender or the other has received so many wounds as to be unable to continue."

"That could be for hours!"

She looked in the direction of the witnesses to this horror, all of them male as far as she could discern, and all suddenly displaying fresh excitement.

Almost against her will, Pamela's eyes darted to the irregular square. Ernest Osset, the legendary Bermondsey Bleeder, his face drenched in claret enough for the contents of a vineyard, had slid to one knee. The Knightsbridge Knave, lips curled contemptuously, stepped away as if disowning his handiwork.

"It must be finished now!" Pamela said huskily. "He can no longer stand!"

"Bermondsey would have to strike the ground lengthwise and be asleep in public, so to speak, for the struggle to be finished beforehand. As it is, he is only taking a rest within the confines of a round. The procedure is frowned on but permitted to a contender in some distress."

"It prolongs the slaughter." Pamela nodded rigidly in proof that her intelligence was no longer moribund. "Never could I have imagined any proceeding like this!"

"I should hope not," the Earl agreed.

"I am unable to comprehend why you have brought me here, your lordship, but this massacre must be halted immediately in the name of humanity and decency."

"Do you have any plan in mind for achieving so worthy a goal?"

Pamela spoke decisively. "I do indeed."

She was reaching to the door of the carriage when she suddenly felt his hand over hers. He must have moved with the celerity of the Knightsbridge Knave's left thumb, an appendage whose dexterity had made that pugilist a byword, as she was eventually to be told.

"Let me go!" she demanded. "I will run out to that square and demand the slaughter be stopped! It is intolerable that such a grisly spectacle be allowed for one moment in a land that calls itself civilized."

Kinnon said nothing, but she wondered if his head had moved in the beginnings of a nod. Perhaps a trick of torchlight had deceived her.

"If I cannot leave this carriage immediately, I will shout for my freedom."

"Because of the clamor without," Kinnon remarked, "no one who could help will hear."

She wasn't going to be permitted to leave. Aware of that much, and of a tingle on the back of one lightly gloved hand, she pulled back. Kinnon's palm promptly detached itself from the contact with her.

"Any man worth his salt would put a stop to this horror," she insisted.

A collective sigh, perhaps of disappointment, came from the fiends in attendance at this *danse macabre.* Pamela, once more taking advantage of the height afforded by the carriage, looked out only long enough to see both gladiators turn their backs on each other and proceed weakly to opposite corners.

"As you see, the affray has come to a pause." Kinnon's narrowed eyes raked the surroundings, however, which surprised Pamela without her knowing why.

Although he glanced back to assure himself that she remained in place, he spoke loudly to someone on the ground.

"How've you been, Terry?" asked the Earl.

"Ah, I thought it was you in the carritch, yer ludship," said a cockney voice. "I comes over to make sure."

Glancing out over Kinnon's shoulder, Pamela saw a toothless man with a wide smile and rumpled clothes.

"Is the best coiner in London still on that lay?" the Earl asked.

"Not so's you'd know it any more, yer ludship."

"Why not?"

"A few years at public school," the coiner said, using what was probably thieves' cant for prison, "an' me stumps got broken by a bloody warder." He lifted his hands, showing fingers that seemed to have been reshaped into claws.

"Can't do no coinin' wiv these. Can 'ardly do mout else any more."

"Don't you have a lay now?"

"I 'elps me friend Ernie, you know, when 'e ain't bleedin'." Presumably his friend was Ernest Osset himself, known in song and story as Bermondsey.

Pamela looked away and settled back. No doubt Terry had observed her out of the corner of an eye, but he made no comment. The lady friends of a peer were a law unto themselves, in the cockney's view.

It crossed her mind, too, to ask herself how a peer should come to have made the acquaintance of a counterfeiter. A gentleman, though, was likely to venture into different classes of society, using the freedom that was granted by virtue of his gender. A man like Kinnon, who involved himself with the workings of Parliament, was more likely than most to have made prolonged contacts in various strata. Very possibly, too, he would be more keenly aware of inequities unlike those that had been agitating her for so long.

"Yes, I remembered that you're a friend of the Berm—of Ernie." Kinnon took one more look back at her, gesturing with a finger for her to remain in place. "I would like to talk with you."

"Certainly, me ludship," said Terry. "I will be 'appy to make meself available."

Kinnon may have smiled in response. He reached for the knob, opened the carriage door, and jumped down, closing the door partway behind him.

Left alone for however brief a period, Pamela's thoughts were occupied almost entirely by the prospect of stopping the brutal fray that would soon be continuing. At this time, however, the groundlings were so firmly involved with heated conversation, presumably in the course of making wagers on the outcome, that she wouldn't be heard.

One of the men soon began walking up and down the irregular-square battleground, a palm raised to capture the attention of those others who were present. No doubt the murder was to resume as soon as his wish for attention was met. With it, though, would come an approximation of silence. Never would she have a better opportunity to attempt the saving of a man's very life.

She was aware of the door on the other side abruptly opening. Kinnon had returned. There was a moment when she might have made her exit from the carriage after all, but would have perhaps been in some danger had she done so amid the turmoil and would almost certainly be caught up by Kinnon and prevented from doing what was of the greatest importance. The only sound in the carriage for a brief time was that of her teeth gnashing.

Kinnon, smiling, finally said, "This is not the best possible location in which a young lady could take a stroll."

"I will never see or speak with you again," she responded. "I cannot abide a man without the courage of the convictions he has indicated he shares with me, a man who is a coward and a poltroon."

Kinnon seemed unaffected by the threat or the rebuke. His attitude resembled that of Pamela's aunt explaining to the family physician that the niece was far too sensitive to ingest any medicine, no matter how effectively it might relieve some distress or other.

"In that case, Miss Pamela, it behooves me to experience the pleasure of your company until the battle is concluded."

She sat back, eyes stubbornly shut.

The fray almost certainly resumed, judging

from the loud calls of the groundlings encouraging the contenders to commit various acts of mayhem upon each other's person. The shouts rose almost to roars and were followed by a wave of angry exclamations that were as surprising as they were vehement.

Despite her previous intentions, Pamela opened her eyes. The sight that confronted her caused her to blink several times and even to shake her head as if wanting to clear it urgently.

The impossible had happened. Ernest Osset, the Bermondsey Bleeder himself, stood in the center of the ring. Although the battle was supposed to be under way by this time, he was unimpeded. It was the other battler, the so-called Knightsbridge Knave, the one who was known far and wide for underhanded tactics, who had been bested. Knightsbridge lay silently off center on the ground. His eyes were closed. A while ago, Kinnon had indicated that the battle would end abruptly if one of the contenders was asleep in public. The Knightsbridge Knave was meeting that condition handsomely.

"There has been an advance in time for the predetermined outcome to be reached," Kinnon said. "It was intended that money be wagered upon Knightsbridge and that the money be lost."

It was in her mind to berate the bet takers for palpable dishonesty, but she spared herself the effort. A shudder racked her.

"You may consider yourself fortunate not to have witnessed a contest between the Mayfair Mangler and the Trafalgar Square Thug," said the Earl of Kinnon. "I think we can leave now."

Pamela sat back, breathing heavily until the scene of this Agincourt-like engagement had been put behind them.

"Are you well?" asked Kinnon softly.

Concern for her was clear in his features, in the drawn-down brows, the inquiring tilt of the head.

"I am better, thank you, your lordship. You did have something to do with the merciful ending of that—that *grotesquerie.*"

"Indeed yes."

He had brought her to the scene in order that his decisiveness might be observed. Like Pamela, he was moved by feelings of compassion but chose not to antagonize others more than necessary in showing them. Nor did he inform anyone in advance of his plans. Keeping his own counsel was, perhaps, part of the reason for his success in the rooms of Parliament. A ship's captain, according to legend, didn't inform any ordinary seaman about necessary changes in course.

"I spoke to Terry, the coiner," Kinnon said.

"Surely you did more than speak." Once again her intelligence had come out of hiding.

"I gave him money enough so that he could keep some for his own services and offer most of it to Ernie for finishing Knightsbridge in short order and concluding the match before either man might be gravely hurt."

"That's wonderful," Pamela said, startled and pleased although she had realized for a while what must have taken place behind the scenes. She ought to have trusted the owner of those probing light gray eyes to make the correct choice.

The carriage halted too soon in Clifford Street. Kinnon descended first. His strong hands aided Pamela in reaching ground at long last.

"We shall see each other again," he said decisively.

There was no dispute offered in this matter.

"I shall write as soon as the press of government matters again permits. But it will not be long, Pamela, if I have to wring Queen Vickie's neck myself to persuade her into doing what is necessary as quickly as may be."

On the disquieting mention of contact with another female, Pamela became aware of his lips approaching hers. She returned the proffered kiss with the greatest alacrity. It would not have mattered in the least whether Aunt Rosemary or Ian or even Hope were to glance out of a window and witness the proceeding.

Only reluctantly did his lips part from hers and his arms withdraw from her back. She had been aware of the pressure thus elicited without identifying it, and now she wondered if she could keep from removing this dress for many hours.

He turned and climbed into the carriage once more. Pamela watched his departure.

CHAPTER 13
The Discharge of an Obligation

Mr. Dickon Granbrook had solemnly informed Pamela how he felt about her flouting of a respected elder's expressed wishes. As a longtime friend of the late Uncle Vincent's, this primary force in the construction of the celebrated Castlerigg to Buttermere Railway took it upon himself to show dismay. There was every sign of the anger that was often present in his reddened features, but he was tamping it down as best he could. Mrs. Granbrook had probably insisted on his doing so.

"I consider that you led my Dilys to make a fool of herself," he added as the family and two guests settled down in the Granbrook suite at the Wimmer to have a quiet supper. Or as quiet as could be managed with Mr. Granbrook on the verge of eruption.

Dilys said sullenly, "Pamela has been my best friend in the world."

"Your best friend," said Mrs. Granbrook, interceding before her husband could speak, "has offered a horrible example as to how a young woman should behave."

"Pammie has done the right thing in refusing to marry at someone else's insistence!"

"Bah!" On the point of giving way, Mr. Granbrook glanced at his wife and drew back. "You must look for guidance to those who are older than you."

There was no reason whatever to point out that Pamela at eighteen was a year older than the shy Dilys. Aunt Rosemary, a spoon poised over the mock turtle soup, looked from Pamela to their host but wisely kept the thought to herself.

Mrs. Granbrook said soothingly, "Dilys, my baby, you have to be very careful when it comes to judging others. Trust your mother to show you the proper direction."

Dilys sulked, remembering that her mother had found complaints against any girl whom Dilys called a friend, even the richest, the prettiest, and the smartest. Dilys could only speak with her friends from home at local parties and then only for a little while. Customarily she found that proceeding to be deliciously sinful because she knew that her parents would sternly disapprove.

"If you are going to let yourself be courted by a ragamuffin," Mr. Granbrook began, speaking firmly and censoriously to his only child.

"He's not that!" Dilys was impelled to respond, then looked around awkwardly in embarrassment at her outburst.

"Pray watch your tongue, miss!" her father snapped, deftly making the word "pray" sound like the most horrible of anathemas. "I was saying that I must therefore earn sufficient moneys to support the two of you."

"Father, I beg of you not to think of Mr. Holt in that way!"

"Be silent, young woman!" Mr. Granbrook paused to collect such corollary thoughts as had discovered refuge within his brain. "I will apparently have to take the first opportunity to abandon my conservative and proper management of a burgeoning enterprise."

Mrs. Granbrook put in, "Now do you realize, my baby, to what lengths your stubbornness could drive your own dear father?"

Pamela, a witness to her friend's humiliation, wanted to speak up on Dilys' behalf. She could swiftly have said that Mr. Granbrook had never met Avery Holt and didn't know whether or not he would be a suitable son-in-law. Further,

Avery was a solicitor and disarmingly respectable. Not wealthy, true, not a peer, but no one would have to look the other way at a prospect of his becoming a family connection. Nobody, that is, except a *nouveau riche* like Uncle Vincent's friend. It was most unfortunate that Dilys herself, in an access of feeling, had told her parents about having met and been affected by this ornament of the Queen's Bench.

For Pamela to speak up, however, would give far more ammunition to Dickon Granbrook, enabling him to conclude beyond doubt and in complete disregard of factual content that his daughter's friend had indeed corrupted her. Better to endure this folly as best she could, following the recent example of Kinnon in a difficulty. At a later time, surely, she could offer aid and comfort to Dilys.

"I would have to sell my interest in the railroad," Mr. Granbrook said with overdone regret that indicated he would do nothing of the sort. His dramaturgy must have sounded insincere even to the ears of the serving staff whose members were diligently at work in this rented dining room. "A sale after some period of sound footing would bring in enough money to keep your mother and myself in the barest comfort.

The outgo to support you and your impoverished commoner of a prospective husband, not to mention any issue that might accumulate as a result of that miserable union you envisage, would put us into pauperdom."

"But he is not a poor man!"

"Whilst I am in London I may make inquiries to see if the sale can be consummated, and to find quarters for your mother and myself in one of the more squalid areas of the city. We will not be able to afford any other accommodation from now on because of you."

The consideration of poverty came at a time when one of the serving girls was handling the remove, carrying a great quantity of mutton haunch. No one gave any assistance, although the weight seemed more than one girl could handle.

"With the Empire on the brink of great expansion," Dickon Granbrook was saying, even more pointedly than usual, "it would be a tragedy to—what the *devil!*"

The dish of mutton haunch had been tilted dangerously down in his direction.

The girl said pacifically, "I'm very sorry, sir."

"Sorry? Sorry, is it! Why, you could have done great damage to this suit and made it impossible for me to wear it ever again, let alone causing me the greatest discomfort."

"I'm sure I'm very sorry, Mr. Granbrook," the girl said once more, speaking quickly.

"You shall be even sorrier," said the choleric railroad entrepreneur, his normally red face darkening further. "I shall see to it that you *are* sorrier."

Mrs. Granbrook, taking it upon herself to keep her husband's furies in check, said abruptly to the girl, "You are to leave immediately and you will not be paid for the night's work. Out!"

Mr. Granbrook himself looked a little astonished by vehemence from an unexpected source.

It was the last word which infuriated Pamela to a point of no return. Lips pursed, eyes narrowed, she surged to her feet. The self-imposed reminder that Kinnon might have been more tactful had no effect now.

"You are condemning this girl to a possible life on the streets!"

Aunt Rosemary spoke her name once, but it was useless. As for Dickon Granbrook, his eyes widened in astonishment. Never before had he seen a young woman turn angrily upon an elder.

Coldly Pamela said, "You owe that girl a reference if you discharge her! The life of a working girl without one is hardly worth living."

Mrs. Granbrook, herself a woman beyond question, had heard tales of the plight of females dismissed out of hand. She nodded almost in spite of herself. Justice of a sort, Pamela felt, would be done.

Mr. Granbrook was incensed, however. "I refuse to discuss this," he said, his voice resembling muffled thunder. He slapped his palms against the table top. "There has been enough of this!"

"Indeed there has," Pamela agreed coldly. "Arrogance and bad manners are social abominations."

She turned away. Aunt Rosemary stood, and Pamela started to the door. It would have been unbearable if her aunt had tried to make peace after a night of affronts that had been given not only to her but to a helpless female.

Mr. Granbrook spoke forbiddingly to his daughter. "Dilys, you will see this one no more, ever!"

Aunt Rosemary was following Pamela to the door. Like Pamela, she said no word to the others.

Despite her own very real anger, Pamela felt

cheered by her aunt's support. In praise of Rosemary Forrest, her niece wanted to send up the proverbial three cheers and a tiger.

At the door Pamela glanced back in the direction of Dilys. Their eyes met. Dilys was silently asking for assistance, but Pamela knew that because of her own impetuousness she would almost certainly be unable to offer it ever again.

CHAPTER 14
Love Laughs at Dismay

Dilys didn't cry when she was alone in her room, nor did she permit herself to recall what had taken place at supper. She was occupied with changing into a newly purchased costume. Mother came in to inspect her at just before nine o'clock, an ordeal that had preceded every party that the family had ever attended, and one which Dilys always dreaded.

As usual, at the beginning, Mother was complimentary.

"Most attractive," she said, having asked Dilys to walk up and down. Mother behaved as if she hadn't virtually picked out this demi-basque with its overlapping blond satin flounces on the skirt. "The turquoise goes very well with dark hair and it even helps display your eyes to the best effect. That insertion *is* set attractively and the trimming is fine, but you must be sure that it doesn't catch on anything."

Dilys nodded, waiting apprehensively for the

extra word or two that was certain to make her unhappy, reducing her to tears long afterward.

"It all looks far better than I would have expected and distinctly as though it belongs on a grown woman," Mother decided at last. There was nothing to fault in the voice or tones, but Dilys became convinced that Mother felt it was hopeless to make any changes, hopeless because Dilys was so infernally young.

"But the shoes with such imposing heels!" Mother had at last found an accessory of which she could wholeheartedly disapprove. "A short peer will refuse to consider dancing with you tonight."

Dilys, who had hurriedly purchased the objects because of Avery's great height, had no wish to explain that she would be seeing him at tonight's ball.

"My baby wants to look older," Mrs. Granbrook gushed, conceiving and accepting the only explanation she would have approved. "Very well, if you wish, Dilys dear." She was relieving herself of all responsibility in case Dilys proved unsuccessful in the night's quest for a suitor. "Tomorrow, though, you return to being my baby."

Dilys smiled insincerely. She had no wish

whatever to go back to a position as anyone's helpless baby, not at this time in her life.

Sir Humphrey Packwood, his lady, and their daughter lived in St. John's Wood, not far from Regent's Park. Miss Miriam Packwood, sporting a dress that was more full than she herself would ever be, greeted them at her mother's side in the so-called grand saloon of the house. The two girls weren't close friends. Indeed an invitation had been extended only because Sir Humphrey and the late Vincent Forrest had been of such assistance to Mr. Dickon Granbrook in accomplishing his life's work of having a railroad built in Cumberland. Neither of the elder Granbrooks considered that they owed this night's husband-catching opportunity for their daughter to the shrewdness of Mrs. Rosemary Forrest's late husband and uncle of the infernal Pamela.

Certainly the Forrests wouldn't be attending this festivity. A wit in the great tradition of the late Mr. George Brummell had remarked that it would be impossible tonight to see the Forrests for the debris. It was a remark that Mr. Granbrook wouldn't have understood at all, and several of that local wit's auditors, it may be added, had looked puzzled as well.

Dark draperies on the sides of this room showed the other girls' dresses to some effect. Dilys confronted a tense image of herself in the pier glass not far from a marble bust of the self-assured Queen. An orchestra at the north end of this room was starting to play popular selections. Young males and females had planted themselves in separate corners and were engaging in conversation, as if wanting to make it plain that they hadn't come here to do anything so *déclassé* as to confront members of the opposite sex. Chaperones, many dressed in pink and white, busied themselves in conversation at a midpoint between the two camps.

It did seem at the start that males had to be dragooned into doing their social duty. Dilys found herself doing a Caledonian with a pimpled youth whom Mother didn't discourage, a mazurka with a blond cross-eyed lad, and a polka with a much older man who danced well but whose eyes roamed right and left all the time.

"We must refuse more dances," said Mrs. Granbrook, "now that you look flushed as a result of being on the floor and have proven yourself to be popular. From now on, you dance only with a titled man who is in the position to make you happy."

Dilys supposed that Mother would indeed be helpful and encouraging until a suitor appeared, and then she would become recalcitrant at knowing that proof of her own advancing age was palpable and that she might soon become a grandmother.

It was impossible not to see Avery Holt in the room. He towered over all of them. At sight of her, his eyes appeared to light up, which was certainly encouraging.

He approached smilingly. "I have come to claim a dance."

Mrs. Granbrook was inquiring but didn't disapprove. Avery's height appeared to make him sufficiently unsuitable so that her baby wouldn't shame her by marrying, not quite yet.

Nonetheless, Dilys was unprepared to chance a possible maternal frown.

"Your lordship can certainly dance with me."

A confused Avery was led out to the floor, although he apparently considered that he was taking matters in hand himself.

"My mamma will permit you to dance with

me if she thinks that you are a peer," she explained before he could raise the question.

Avery looked puzzled but didn't make any remark about it. Dear man though he was, he seemed very slightly lacking in imagination.

"You dance beautifully, as I might expect," he said, confirming yet again that she had made a conquest. "You have the great self-assurance that a girl with your comeliness should indeed have."

Was that what he thought of her? He was a dear, the very dearest of dears. Her heart was hammering against her chest. She seemed, for a moment, to see nothing but dots pulsing on a field of red.

She danced proudly, with head erect, looking straight in front of her rather than gazing far up to remind him yet again how tall he was. She liked his touch, cool but not sweaty. She wanted him to put his hands in different places later on. The very thought made her flush. None like it had ever come to her before. The words "wifely duties" were spoken softly by some inner voice as if referring to a great and wonderful pleasure.

Her accelerated height allowed her to look over one of Avery's shoulders in the course of dancing. A slow *valse* brought Mr. and Mrs.

Granbrook into her view, and the beginnings of disquiet as well.

She could see Mamma and Pappa engaged in conversation with each other. Mamma's head was inclined toward the area in which couples disported themselves at dance. Pappa suddenly looked into her eyes, then turned and spoke to a neighbor. That man responded, perhaps identifying Avery Holt as a man without a title, a mere solicitor, the son of a father whose sneezing fits were fast making him a figure of mythic proportions in London society.

"It won't be long before we are interrupted," Dilys said reluctantly.

"By whom?"

Avery was apparently so pleased with the close contact of his love that he had forgotten the information that had been passed on to him only moments ago.

"By my esteemed elders," Dilys said, and it was impossible to know whether or not a tinge of sarcasm had crept into her tones. "They will have been apprised that you are not a peer."

"Oh. Oh yes." Avery spared a glance over his shoulder. The Granbrooks were advancing purposefully in the direction of the area that had been sequestered for dancing.

"The next few moments might be unpleasant if you don't release me and make for the exit at a dignified lope."

"This is not fair," Avery complained. The Granbrooks, nothing loath to create a scene in public, were encroaching upon the outer rim of dancers. Mr. Granbrook, never famed for the evenness of his temper, had contorted his features, and they looked almost as flame-red as the innards of a railroad car on the Castlerigg-to-Buttermere route.

It was this crisis which brought out the best in Avery Holt. British pluck of the sort that was winning an empire in the Queen's name could have boasted no greater exemplar than this oversized solicitor in the next moment.

"I must make sure that you won't forget me," he said doggedly.

Dilys felt his hand venture under her chin. Startled by the touch, she looked up at his handsome face. He was breathing with difficulty, and his act was purposeful. Without losing a step or breaking the rhythm of the dance, his lips descended upon hers and she was being kissed as never before. It didn't occur to Dilys that she ought to break away in the name of propriety, nor would she have done so if the thought had crossed her mind.

It seemed that every man and woman in sight suddenly gave vent to a collective gasp of astonishment, every male pausing in the quest of a woman, every woman almost distracted from the task of working her wiles on some man with the intent of ensnaring his fealty for life.

Dilys was aware of being released. She focused her newly opened eyes upon the sight of Avery walking at a brisk pace away from the dance area. In his own excitement he nearly crashed into a maiden with a wafer-thin gown. He apologized hastily and reeled away, remaining upright only with prodigious effort.

Dilys raised three fingers to her lips and had blown a kiss at him by the time Mamma and Pappa reached her.

CHAPTER 15
Contretemps at the Zoo

"I am not sure that my advice will be welcome," Aunt Rosemary began.

"Indeed it is," Pamela insisted. "I should not have to say so in my eighteenth year."

"You are no longer a child, true," Aunt Rosemary said thoughtfully, having heard little of Pamela's disclaimer. "To an aunt, her only niece, the niece she raised, is always a child in memory."

It was a sentiment with which a vain woman such as Olympia Granbrook would have agreed, but only in part. Pamela smiled in what she hoped was an agreeable manner.

"My advice would be not to make a cause of the Dilys Granbrook matter," Aunt Rosemary said. "It is unfortunate, let us agree, but your fulminations can do nothing to remedy this injustice."

Pamela found it easy to understand Aunt Rosemary's point of view. Her aunt was a product of that cast of mind which held that civilization was advanced solely by the male and that a woman of whatever age was powerless to thwart the wishes of the supreme sex. It was a concept with which Pamela, as has been made clear, wholly disagreed.

Her aunt had been upset to hear from Miriam Packwood during a casual meeting that there had been an upset regarding Miss Dilys Granbrook at some time during the ball that the Packwoods had given on the previous night, the ball to which she had been forbidden to invite Pamela and her aunt. Miriam, though a contemporary of Pamela's, had spoken to the aunt almost as freely as she might have spoken to the niece.

This news and the attendant advice had been communicated to Pamela as soon as was feasible. The young woman reacted strongly.

"I must speak with Dilys or Avery," she said, having given the matter some thought. "One or the other is certain to be at the Gardens this afternoon."

She was referring, as Aunt Rosemary well knew, to the Gardens of the Zoological Society of London. Not since the association had been founded by Sir Stamford Raffles with the valuable assistance of Sir Humphrey Davy had the establishment been so popular. Hardly a day seemed to pass without the arrival of some beasts unlike any that had been hitherto observed in the purlieus of London. On this afternoon it was planned to exhibit several newly arrived sea lions. The picturesqueness of that name was enough by itself to insure a diversified attendance by Fashionables and their camp followers.

The invaluable canoe landau of the Forrests proceeded to that park area in which the zoo buildings could be discerned among several surprisingly scrawny trees. Once they had passed through the main entrance, Pamela and her aunt soon discovered an almost animal-like variety of zoo attendee, a new species in itself. Pamela, highly visible in her dark poke bonnet and small-waisted dark merino day dress covered in part by a dotted lilac shawl, saw no sign of Avery or Dilys in the multitude.

Nor was either to be seen among those observing the black sea lions who made a sound that resembled, to her ears, that of Mr. Dickon Granbrook under stress. The reptile house was equally bereft of Avery or Dilys if not of salamanders and pythons and their ilk. The monkey house was, as ever, a scene of cheer, the rodent house a scene of pseudo-religious speculation, the lion house a site for the awe of various spectators. Upon emerging from this latter habitation Pamela encountered the Earl of Kinnon deep in conversation with three men.

She called out inadvertently, causing Kinnon to turn and ask her and Aunt Rosemary to join them. A look of pleasure lightened his serious aspect.

The smallest of these strangers was introduced to a suddenly weakened Pamela, who could hardly concentrate her faculties long enough to show the expected courtesies. This was Mr. Dickens, the novelist. The bearded one was Mr. Longfellow, a poet from America. Mr. Longfellow spoke the common language as if he had read it in a book but never pronounced the words until this occasion. The third, a grim-faced man with yellowed teeth and his head thrown back, was not a figure of celebrity. Pamela didn't retain the name once she heard it. Aware of her indifference, he promptly resumed the conversation at the point it had reached before Pamela and her aunt were intruded upon them.

"As I tell you, gentlemen," he said pompously, "these are good times."

"To some, they are bad times," Kinnon contradicted in part, with a look of apology at Pamela and her aunt for not giving them more of his attention.

"Good times, but also bad times," said Mr. Dickens, ruminating aloud. "*There* is a phrase which might be turned to account in the pages of a novel."

Mr. Dickens and his friend soon departed, the former murmuring, "These are good times and also bad times—no, that doesn't have quite the grandiloquence, my dear Longfellow, which I would prefer."

Kinnon, in a canary waistcoat and tight trousers, had come out to the zoo on a mission of some importance, it soon transpired. In partnership with a friend, he had purchased a substantial interest in the *Half-Penny News,* one of the four-sheet papers which dealt in society scandals as fodder for publication. This course had apparently been decided upon as a result of Pamela's recent travails, judging from his speech and the glances he ventured in her direction.

He sounded like a man determined upon change, in this case to have the newspaper become more responsive to the political currents of the age. Such a maneuver would at the same time offer Kinnon and his friend a platform for airing their views publicly without accusations that they might encounter if such views were directly attributed to them.

"I think that the nation is getting a bit above itself in making it clear to the world that we are dealing with the Turks and the Tsar," he added. "And I don't know, truly, that we should suddenly become such good friends with the French."

"Arggh!" the other said pensively. "Our readers is only interested in reading 'bout Society and sports, and some about British heroes and new atrocities committed by the wogs."

Pamela couldn't help intruding, her voice puzzled. "But who would they be?"

"Wogs is another word for foreigners, Miss, of any stripe or color. Anything else in the paper and they look elsewhere."

"If other inducements are offered, they might not do so," Kinnon said stubbornly.

It soon became clear that the Earl had made further plans to alter and hopefully improve the paper. Its price would rise and its title accordingly become the *Penny News*. Fresh events would be written up each day, and articles were to be surrounded with more space. The other, experienced in the folkways of journalism, distastefully referred to the added space as "wider gutters."

Further, it appeared that Kinnon and his colleague wanted the paper to pay for some news, insisting that some member of the staff interview anyone who claimed to offer an important news item that might not have appeared elsewhere. With the backing of an informant who could earn at least a shilling for coveted information, the paper would increase its reputation as a source of news. Once that was done, the opinion and speculation it would now be offering about world affairs and national politics would gain accordingly in credibility.

"We will get a fierce amount of bamming," the other objected.

"Money won't be issued until the Monday after our paper has appeared."

Further objections were made and answered or brushed to one side.

Pamela, listening intently at first, found herself growing angry at the Earl. Clearly his interest in change was limited to matters of world policy or national policy. Not the slightest interest did he show in matters of injustice which plagued British females such as herself and

Dilys. He was virtually sailing the world while suffering was commonplace in his own native land.

The burgher with yellow teeth eventually smiled at Pamela and Aunt Rosemary, then walked off into a grove of sickly-looking trees. One of the sea lions let out a bellow, whether at sight of him or not it was impossible to ascertain.

Over the sounds of this commotion, Pamela began speaking more snappishly than her aunt for one would have advised. "Have you heard about the difficulties of your good friend Avery Holt?"

Kinnon, recalled to issues far more mundane in his view, nodded. Disappointment shaded his eyes as he had expected to speak with her about matters involving the pleasures of flirtation. Such shilly-shallying would have helped confirm their good feelings for one another. Pamela Forrest's voice seemed almost to have deepened with indignation checked by the greatest difficulty. A glow appeared at her cheekbones almost like paint, and her lips were as moist-looking as if they had been dipped into a pot. He was aware of anger he had done nothing to provoke.

"Is that all you can do?" Pamela looked startled as well as angry. "A horror is perpetrated in society and you can only nod your head to acknowledge it."

He was driven to sarcasm. "Do you expect that I will take a hall and intone fiery speeches about a thwarted romance?"

"You could perform less responsive acts."

"If you consider that making the attempt to sway British policy by soliciting public approval is an irrelevant act," he said, snappish in return, "then we are in strong disagreement."

"It is not the most important deed that could be done by you at this time."

Aunt Rosemary interceded quietly. "If I may be permitted to say so, I am able to see his lordship's point, Pamela, as well as yours. I have not the slightest idea what you would expect his lordship to do."

"The Earl of Kinnon ought to take sides without losing the good will of any participants and see to it that his friend (and my own two friends) achieve the happiness together for which they are palpably aching."

"How do you propose that I accomplish the feat?" Kinnon asked.

"As to that, I cannot say. I do know that I

have been exposed by you to more than one peroration about the necessity to accomplish change in a manner that disturbs none and results in happiness for all."

"Indeed," Kinnon said, perhaps in agreement that wasn't entirely necessary.

"The methods with which to accomplish this, your lordship, have eluded me up to the moment. I sit at your feet accordingly."

The Earl blushed, and Pamela was taken aback by the strength of his reaction.

"I am a student of the Earl's, and I wish to see how my preceptor could bring about the desired conclusion in the matter with which we are occupied."

"You cannot expect me to interfere in a situation of this type!"

"I can and do," Pamela insisted. "It is an excellent way to demonstrate to me the effectiveness of your theories."

"It also offers a splendid chance to discomfit several strangers."

"As Mr. Charles Dickens might have written if someone had said it to him first, 'One cannot construct an omelet without first pulverizing eggs.'"

"My dear Miss Forrest—Pamela, you must

not think of me as a genie from the lamp," Kinnon protested. "If you rub the lamp correctly with the prescribed number of strokes, the genie will not necessarily appear and grant your every wish."

"Can you not right a major wrong like this one?"

"In the context of world problems, this is more of an *opéra comique*, but you anticipate that I will become exercised over it."

Aunt Rosemary, having involuntarily been a listener to the continuation of this verbal affray, drew a soft breath. Plainly she desired to contribute yet again to the course of the discussion.

Kinnon politely turned to her.

"Your lordship, I ask you to believe that no woman is able or permitted to deal with problems of British policy (there is, of course, a royal exception to that rule, but we need not discuss her). To a woman, domestic difficulties take the place of such diversions, and I use the latter word because the movements of great masses are different from the behavior of small groups in one's immediate area of activity. If a woman marries unhappily, her entire life will be altered for the worse. Let a man marry unhappily, and he can deal with others by day and not return home until late at night, as you are surely aware."

"I acknowledge the justice of what you say," Kinnon conceded slowly, with a look at Pamela to indicate that the argument should have been mounted from the first with so skillful a combination of tact and forcefulness. Aunt Rosemary was apparently a dedicated advocate of Kinnon's methods, although in a smaller arena.

Something of the same thought had now occurred to the peer. "It seems to me that you would be able to suggest numerous methods for resolving the difficulty."

Pamela said explosively, "It is not a 'difficulty,' as you patronizingly call it! The future of a woman is involved, her happiness on this earth is involved!"

Aunt Rosemary, however, spoke directly to the challenge that had been offered. "Let us accept it that your compliments about my acuity are deserved, although I would not directly acknowledge it in so many words. Still, I am not able to speak with the major participants in this matter. Young Avery Holt I could certainly approach, but not the Granbrooks. And not in any way would I be allowed a moment's congress with Dilys. I might add that Pamela finds herself in substantially the same position."

"You are therefore suggesting that I seek out these strangers?" Kinnon's fraying temper was not improved by the expostulations of an irritable duck not far away. "I am unacquainted with them. There is no reason under the sun for those people to listen as I urge them to permit their daughter to plight her troth with a commoner."

Looking at him through the haze of her own anger, Pamela was aware that he was handsome as the Devil himself. She wondered how many other females appreciated his appearance as much as she herself did.

"If you cannot devise a *modus vivendi* to help someone you have called a friend in the course of a great difficulty, your lordship, then what good is a philosophy such as yours? The purpose of any philosophy of life, it seems to me, is not to permit injustice to rule your existence or that of those of whom you may be fond."

His intense light gray eyes seemed fastened on Pamela's lips as if to drain every intonation from them.

"And you would scorn me because of this one matter," he said.

Was the monster actually smiling? It did not occur to Pamela that he might be feeling rue in regard to the error he had made over this aspect of dealing with her.

"Scorn, yes, because you have spoken so much nonsense to me over the recent days."

"In that case, permit me to bid you a good afternoon," he said abruptly, retreating from further discussion. Similar sentiments were offered to a bemused Aunt Rosemary.

A lion roared, perhaps in sympathy with the peer as he strode away.

Aunt Rosemary, feeling the necessity to make a comment more articulate than the animal's, remarked quietly, "Ian would have enjoyed this excursion."

Pamela, disinclined to give the least thought to her young brother at this moment, looked after Kinnon till the latter disappeared from sight. He didn't look back.

"You seem to have brought this hullabaloo upon yourself," Aunt Rosemary put in with a distinct lack of the quality of mercy. "Apparently, you anticipate no regrets over losing the attentions of the Earl of Kinnon."

Pamela said nothing. Her aunt almost certainly knew from experience with Pamela that the younger female could under no circumstances have behaved in any other manner.

CHAPTER 16
Disappearance and Exile

The trip home was rife with recollections of the meeting just concluded. For some arcane reason the coachman saw fit to pass through that picturesque little street on which newspaper offices were located *en masse*. Folk were strolling back and forth from one row of bulletins to another, as if the news itself would be altered on different hoardings in front of publication offices.

To observe the nightly ritual of supper, Pamela changed into a simple black dress that seemed to expand her features so relentlessly that she didn't often wear it on other than family occasions. Aunt Rosemary began the meal after grace by suggesting the possibility that Kinnon be invited to forage with them on another night this week. Over the trough, as she put it, the possibility might be cleared for a *rapprochement* between herself and Kinnon.

As the subject proved lacking in popularity, Aunt Rosemary launched into a discussion about yet another recent attempt by Parliament to impose death duties on the estates of wealthy men. Her reveries about the difficulty of doing Bobby Peel out of death duties, if such were adopted, were not sufficiently striking to keep Pamela's interest. Ian listened in a condition of total apathy, permitting much of his food to remain untasted until Aunt Rosemary issued a peremptory message to him.

A family night was contemplated by Aunt Rosemary in order to divert Pamela from recollections of the day's turmoil. To spur this self-imposed entertainment, Aunt Rosemary began by launching a full-bodied assault upon the piano. Pamela acquitted herself reasonably well in song. Ian read aloud from a book of instruction about the pressing matter of obtaining crickets and cricket cages from faraway Burma. It was not the most successful family night in the Forrests' history, but it was concluded by nine o'clock.

Gratefully, Ian closed his door in the room that had long ago been allotted to him, the room whose possession always seemed a victory. He touched his most valuable property, the lory bird he had been given. To pat its head shortly after entering the room, or so he had firmly convinced himself, was to be granted good luck, to be part of a romantic and faraway place rather than the home in which he was being raised.

The black dress served Pamela once again on the next morning. Aunt Rosemary reminded her that it was necessary to attend the funeral of a longtime servant of the family, one who had been put on pension seven years ago.

Agatha Stroud, the deceased, had arranged for burial at the impressive churchyard of St. Margaret Patten's in Rood Lane. The widower, with whom Pamela was not acquainted, sat as if bent over to half his size. Children of the late Agatha Stroud's lined the front pew in remarkable numbers. No one could look at the survivors without considering some rewards of a long-lasting marriage.

Pamela returned home with her aunt by early afternoon, where she discovered a letter that exacerbated her feelings even further. A friend of her youth, a young male named Daniel Easton, had married a French girl and taken himself across the Channel to live with her. Correspondence with Pamela had been established as he had strong recollections of her concern for the woes of men and women without advantages of birth. She would be interested, more than most, in knowing about life as it was lived in France.

At first he and his Babette had found the going very difficult, it seemed. "We are living in a small flat in the Rue Galande on the Left Bank of Paris, which is all that we can afford."

(Pamela, reading this, conjured up images of the lives of a newly married couple, the holding of hands, the outings, the random pleasures.)

Daniel had found work within a short time, unsatisfactory though it may have been. "In this shop, artificial flowers are manufactured. Like many Parisians, the gaffer is interested in reform with the proviso that his own enterprise and the rhythm of his life are not affected. I rather like him. He reminds me of my father."

Of course Daniel was planning to leave his current situation. "I have made a friend named Dartois, who works on a newspaper called *Le Boulevardier*. I speak to him about English life and he pays me a small stipend, then writes an article for his paper. When it appears, my dear Babette explains it to me and I make notes about it. Someday, if ever I can master this infernal language, I shall write my own articles."

(Pamela was hardly surprised at the mention of newspapers as a crucial factor in someone else's life. It seemed appropriate, somehow, that everything should remind her of the recent passage at arms with Kinnon.)

Not surprisingly, Daniel Easton had evolved a compromise. "I plan to write an article in English, however, and then my dear wife will translate it. The first attempt is to deal with Ascot, in which the French show considerable interest."

As if to rub salt in Pamela's wounds, Daniel Easton added a discussion of French newspapers as opposed to the ones in Bulldom. "As far as I can learn, there has never been a tax on the local product and its manufacturers are more free, as a result, to criticize their rulers. Opportunities in Paris for a journalist are limited, but many of the surrounding towns are shy of newspapers reflecting their own concerns. It causes *mal de mer* of the brain just to think about the possible business opportunities, say in the village of Saint-Germain-en-Laye, which lies fifteen miles from Paris."

For once, Pamela put down a letter unfinished.

There was, however, an added sheet. This had been written upon by Babette Easton, as Daniel's wife correctly signed herself. "Dear Sister Pamela, I have wanted to write you, but had not yet begun to learn the English so well. Now that I may write, permit me to state the hope that you are in good health. I remain yours affectionately, Babette."

The young matron's understanding of English was still not without imperfections, but Pamela felt disinclined to consider these.

"At times everything conspires against one," Pamela informed her aunt, replacing the sheets in the huge girdle that had carried them across the Channel. "With your permission, I will take Hope with me on an outing to the Serpentine. Fresh air will do me some good, I feel quite certain."

Not long afterward she would recall that in the course of the ensuing carriage ride she had given thought to paying a visit to Avery Holt at his chambers in Lincoln's Inn Fields. Several considerations had weighed against that measure. Avery was not always available without an appointment, being often occupied with Silks, which had, in his case, nothing important to do with garments. True, too, she might have encountered Avery's perpetually sneezing progenitor, the sainted Cecil, who retailed gossip with the alacrity of a fishwife. It was better by far to content herself with a brief stroll by the water-side.

She did compose a missive to Avery upon her return, asking for an interview at his earliest convenience. At that time she would commiser-ate with him upon the difficulty caused by the Granbrook elders and volunteer her services as Cupid's aide-de-camp in any capacity whatever. One difficulty about such an offer, well-inten-tioned though it was, consisted, as has been re-marked, of her inability to reach Granbrooks large or small. Nonetheless it was urgent to make her sympathies unmistakably clear.

As it happened, the situation altered within the half hour.

It was seven-thirty, and the family was gath-ered in the large sitting room downstairs, prepa-ratory to the serving of supper. Aunt Rosemary, occupied by knitting, had just laid aside her ber-lin wool and the needles. Ian, released from the day's efforts by his tutor, Mr. Gernald, walked impatiently up and down, which was one of the releases of energy which Aunt Rosemary permit-ted. He had acquired the habit from Uncle Vin-cent, so that she gave a rueful smile when the gavotte commenced and offered no protest.

Pamela, having changed into her Sardinian

blue, found herself thinking that each member of the family, for different reasons, could have said gratefully something like "Sufficient unto the day are the irritations therof." But it was universally admitted that Pamela's point of view about many matters was quite unlike those of others.

It was into this scene of requited happiness that Hope suddenly ventured. An expression of tautness had darkened the generally vacant aspect of the lower housemaid's features.

"What is wrong?" Aunt Rosemary asked, although she felt convinced that supper had been delayed.

"*Entschuldigen Sie*, mum," said the housemaid, her German ancestry coming to the fore unexpectedly, "but there is a gentleman to see you."

"At this time?" Aunt Rosemary was startled by such a display of bad manners. "A gentleman, you say?"

"I think so, mum, though he's terribly excited and won't be put off."

Indeed there was the pounding of footsteps to be heard in the hall. An invader was going to join them momentarily.

Pamela turned to face Kinnon, convinced

that it was the Earl who was about to make an entrance. No doubt he was anxious to ask for Aunt Rosemary to intercede with a willful niece and didn't object if Pamela overheard his plea. It would probably be Kinnon's convoluted idea of a way to win Pamela's heart. He didn't realize that he had already won it and apparently lost it.

The door opened on Mr. Dickon Granbrook.

In morning coat, with a flower-adorned buttonhole, Mr. Granbrook appeared to expand from the shoes upward, rather like a human topiary garden. His chin was in motion without his having to speak. Pamela, taken aback, observed that there seemed to be tufts of gray in his brows, and these, too, quivered with tension.

For Mr. Granbrook was deeply upset. Always prepared to explode with anger, he now seemed in a position where he desperately wanted to do so but couldn't. Never, in Pamela's experience of him, had the man's breath seemed almost to whistle out of his innards. When he did speak, his voice resembled a sea lion's at the zoo.

"Mrs. Forrest, I most urgently request permission to speak with your niece."

Rather than comment that he had wanted nothing to do with Pamela at the last meeting

of the two families, Aunt Rosemary reacted
sympathetically in the face of his obvious distress. There was nothing in her character of
what Hope might have called *schadenfreude.*

"You have my permission, of course."

"Thank you. Pamela, I demand to know—I
ask to know and will respect any confidence,
whether you have heard from my daughter.
Have you been in communication with Dilys
over the last day?"

"I have not."

"Do you give me your word?"

"I do, and will reinforce it by swearing 'on'
anything or anyone you prefer to name."

Aunt Rosemary turned swiftly to look in her
direction, but seemed satisfied by Pamela's hon-
esty, as ever. Pamela was biting her lower lip in
dismay, Mr. Granbrook's tension being nothing
if not contagious.

"What has happened?" Aunt Rosemary que-
ried at last.

Mr. Granbrook, who had been about to turn
and leave, remained in place. Perhaps he was
moved by this interest in the Granbrook family
despite what he considered as the recent un-
pleasantness.

"This afternoon she went out with her

mother," said Mr. Granbrook, drawing a deep breath into previously constricted lungs. "At the Alhambra Theater, which I think is the name of that infernal place, she suddenly rose and informed Mrs. Granbrook of her need to utilize the—hem!—the facility." He blushed scarlet, or perhaps his face was reddening more deeply than usual.

"That hardly seems like the sort of happening to bring you here," Aunt Rosemary pointed out, irritated by his delay in defining the crux of his dilemma. "Many females have the occasion to use similar facilities at the Alhambra Theater and elsewhere."

"Please permit me to continue." Mr. Granbrook was truly as close to the end of his tolerance as the outskirts of Buttermere was close to the end of his triumphant railway. "Dilys suddenly bent over and kissed her mother. In public, mark you! Kissed her as if saying farewell."

He had looked to the member of his own generation for sympathy despite the brief sarcasm from that source. For Ian he had no more than the most cursory glance.

"She did not return, not even by the conclusion of the performance. Mrs. Granbrook, as you may well imagine, was deeply exercised. She proceeded to the aforementioned facility herself, determined to ascertain whether or not Dilys was at all indisposed."

"And was she?"

"Mrs. Forrest, there was no sign of Dilys! No sign at all!"

"Perhaps she went elsewhere in her illness, not wanting to disturb her dear mother's leisure moments."

"Dilys knows that Mrs. Granbrook would be deeply concerned in any case." Dickon Granbrook drew yet another long breath. "Furthermore no one has any recollection, or so it is claimed, of having seen her."

"So many people attend the theater every day," Pamela ventured to point out.

"Pah!" Dickon Granbrook seemed outraged by this further affront to good sense. "How could anyone not remember having seen Dilys? Impossible, I say! They must every one of them be lying!"

Moved though she may have been at the news of Dilys having disappeared from parental scrutiny, Pamela was nonetheless deeply touched yet again by Mr. Granbrook's firm conviction that Dilys was the loveliest representative of her sex, presumably since the late Cleopatra. He may have been almost a parody of an empire-builder, and certainly he was a braggart who could be deeply intolerant, but the pride he so clearly felt and showed in his daughter was always enough to compensate for those deficiencies of character, certainly in the eyes of the fatherless Pamela.

She would have liked to comfort and reassure him, but nothing she said along those lines would be welcome. Very likely he'd go to his grave convinced that no one but Pamela Forrest was responsible for his daughter's lapses, as he would think of them.

For her own part, however, Pamela had no doubt that Dilys had gathered such faculties together as she could, and then gone out to reach Avery. The likelihood of Dilys having become lost was small indeed. A visit of her own to Avery's chambers earlier this afternoon, such as she had contemplated, might indeed have proved fruitful.

"Anything might have gone wrong," Mr. Granbrook fumed. "This being London, she may have been taken off and no one will ever know where she is or see her again."

Pamela resented the city being blamed in a minor but agitating mystery. It was that feeling alone which kept her silent in the time before another interruption.

Hope had once again materialized. The maid's own concern at sight of the drawn faces in the sitting room caused her to make this communication blessedly brief.

"There is a cabman 'ere to speak with Mr. Granbrook," she said, forgoing the opportunity to practice Teutonic inflections yet again. "At the servants' hentrance, of course."

"Why should a cabman—?" Mr. Granbrook began, aggrieved.

"It would be best, I think, to find out," Aunt Rosemary suggested.

Dickon Granbrook needed no additional urging. With almost a military precision he turned and marched to the outer door.

Pamela, noting the stricken look on her brother's features, glanced at the maid. "See that Master Ian receives his supper."

Aunt Rosemary confirmed that instruction with a nod. A grateful look from Ian was aimed in his sister's general direction.

Pamela was behind Mr. Granbrook as he left the house and marched to the servants' entrance at the right. There was a touch of wind, giving the slightest sway to the branches of those few trees with the temerity to have appeared over the length of Clifford Street.

Observing a carriage at the corner, Mr. Granbrook stared into its interior as best he could, satisfying himself that Dilys could not be located there.

The cabman was a burly Londoner who disregarded the clement weather to work in the uniform of his craft: crushed topper, scarf wound around his throat, dark heavy coat, and thick gloves. The combination on this night didn't seem helpful to his temper.

"Your name Granbrook?" he scowled, suspicious.

"Well? Well? What the devil do you want?"

"I 'as a message from your lady."

"Tell it to me, you fool!"

Perversely the cabman grew calmer in the face of the other's irritation. "Now does yer want to 'ear what I 'as to say or does yer want to slang me?"

Granbrook tamped down the ferocious anger that had been distorting his features.

"Give me the message quickly."

"She says you 'ave to come back to the 'otel on the dot."

"Why?"

"Search me, cully."

"You fool! Can't you even transmit a message?"

"That's all I was told," the cabman snapped. "Now I 'as my cab 'ere, and if you 'op in it won't take long to get you back. Otherwise, you might waste more o' yer volleyble time 'untin' another cab."

"Take me back to the Wimmer promptly."

"That'll be three and six first."

Dickon Granbrook's face resembled nothing so much as a volcano about to explode. Nonetheless, he disgorged the coins as requested.

"I ought ter turn 'round an' see the last o' yer," the cabby said. "But 'op in an' I'll try an' let bygones be."

Granbrook's lips were drawn tight together as he did so. He must have realized that the driver, if further antagonized, could delay the return he sought so urgently.

Pamela asked, "Might I join you?" She was curious to be apprised of the next developments in this matter.

Mr. Granbrook nodded, it having undoubtedly crossed his mind that another native of this hellish community might prove helpful as a consultant in his hour of need.

Aunt Rosemary didn't pause to say that a young woman needed more in the way of external covering for a trip on a June night. Disregarding her own comparable unpreparedness, she simply entered the cab behind her niece.

As the drive got under way it occurred to Pamela that mentioning Avery Holt at a time like this would certainly be unsuitable. Mr. Granbrook would not be receptive to auditing a recital of Avery's varied accomplishments, beginning with his skill as a solicitor—and probably ending with the same asset. The fact of his good nature would win no plaudits either. The same concept must have silently occurred to Aunt Rosemary, for she, too, held her peace.

Perhaps Dilys and Avery had come to the Hotel Wimmer and they could accomplish that task themselves, however. Pamela didn't envy them those first few moments in the company of enraged and frustrated parents. Mr. Granbrook in particular would find it difficult to control his surging emotions. Mrs. Granbrook, after the first moments, would probably resign herself to the inevitable if such it proved to be.

The cabman, inspired by the presence of pieces of eight in his pocket, drove intelligently and well. No time was wasted and every possibil-

ity of delay was skirted. By the time Bruton
Street appeared, Mr. Granbrook already had a
hand on the door and was ready to fling that
door open at the first halt.

As it happened there was a pause just before
the Wimmer Hotel materialized. Mr. Granbrook followed his instincts and took flight.

Left behind, Aunt Rosemary issued directions. "Let us off at the hotel."

The place was a hive of activity. Aunt Rosemary, because of her obvious gentility, only had
to make one request *sotto voce* to the clerk before she was vouchsafed the number of the
Granbrook suite on the second floor. Negotiat-
ing the carpeted stairs offered no difficulty to
aunt or niece.

The door of the Granbrook suite was wide
open. Mr. Granbrook had opened other doors
and was calling out at this time, Dilys' name
rising from the cavern on the nether side of his
lips. As Pamela and her aunt entered the suite,
Pamela courteously closing the door, Mr. Granbrook was returning to the hallway.

"She is not here," he said accusingly.

Olympia Granbrook, quietly dressed as ever,
was nodding as she turned to face him. From
the corner of an eye she had observed Pamela

and Aunt Rosemary in concert as they crossed the threshold.

"You send a cabman after me," Mr. Granbrook began, summing up the happenings of the last minute in case his wife had suddenly become dull-witted and forgotten everything. "You tell him to ask me to return home immediately. And when I do, it promptly develops that Dilys is not here."

"That is true," Mrs. Granbrook had to concede.

"In which case, Olympia, might I therefore ask why you chose to intrude upon and truncate my searches?"

"Because I have heard from our daughter," Mrs. Granbrook said after a moment.

"By message? Give it to me!"

Mrs. Granbrook passed over a letter which had been placed on one of the chairs. "I went into Dilys' room just to look about in my sadness and I discovered this on the pillow. It was intended for us. If we hadn't moved so quickly, we would have discovered it a while ago."

"So she disappeared on purpose," the empire-builder muttered.

Pamela and her aunt spared a moment to glance at each other. This fresh knowledge would at least put a satisfactory end to Dickon Granbrook's blethering about his daughter having been kidnapped by London denizens.

Mr. Granbrook occupied the time fumbling with envelope and foolscap sheet, then belatedly reaching for square-rimmed reading glasses.

"It says," Mr. Granbrook reported, turning to Pamela accusingly, " 'I have gone off to be with the man I adore, the only man for me. I will be with him forever.' "

As if to offer additional proof of Pamela's guilt, he handed the letter across. His statement about the contents had been entirely correct. Pamela noticed a thumbnail-sized place with dried moisture at the bottom of the missive.

"It seems as if she was crying when she wrote this."

Pamela was unaware of any need to explain further that Dilys must have been crying because of an inability to speak with her parents about the matter which occupied her sensibilities more than any other.

Mr. Granbrook's aura of perpetual irritation was softened by what seemed like an appearance of his daughter's unease. He turned away, as if he couldn't meet Pamela's eyes. It was entirely possible that he would involve himself and Mrs.

Granbrook in heated discussions, parceling out blame in his wife's direction because she hadn't obtained the confidence of her own daughter.

Mrs. Granbrook said quietly, "My baby!"

Those were the same words with which she always tried to persuade herself that Dilys was wholly incompetent, and she repeated them at a time when evidence to the contrary was most palpable. Like his wife, Mr. Granbrook was wholly unsympathetic with the daughter's immediate aspirations, a fact which was freshly borne in upon Pamela when the man suddenly glared at her.

Rather than expose herself to quarrels and recriminations, she turned to leave. For the second time in a week, and at the same quarters, Aunt Rosemary showed support by following her.

Mr. Granbrook's voice located both women near the door. "If you see or speak to Miss Dilys Granbrook once again, inform her that she is no longer welcome in any home of Mrs. Granbrook's and mine. Further, we will never speak of her. As far as Mrs. Granbrook and I are concerned, she is among the lost, the eternally lost."

Pamela was on the point of turning to quarrel, enraged by the total unreasonableness of the position being adopted by the parents. At which point, she felt Aunt Rosemary's warning touch between her shoulder blades and resumed her way along the course she had previously set for herself.

CHAPTER 17
An Armed Truce

Another meeting with the Earl of Kinnon seemed unlikely in the immediate future, but it took place on the following night.

By that time Pamela had fully considered the matter by herself and discussed it in detail with Aunt Rosemary. Both females explained to each other that they had independently declined to mention Avery Holt, let alone sing his praises, because the anger of Mr. Granbrook precluded any rational discourse.

For her own part, Pamela indicated her feelings of surprise that her friend, after only two meetings with Avery, admirable though he was, had run off with him. Aunt Rosemary, when the point was first brought up, remarked somberly that no mention of marriage had been made in the epistle left behind for the parents.

This, however, was so appalling to contemplate that even Pamela, well aware of injustices done to women at all levels of society, declined to consider the development and its likely consequences.

Furthermore, as it happened, there was an important supper to be attended on this night and more even than the usual preparations were necessary.

The longtime employees' dinner, for those who had been in the service of the Forrest Bank at least twenty years, was held in the banquet room of Paramore's Oyster Restaurant on the north side of Fetter Lane. Distant cousins of Vincent Forrest's had begun the enterprise, and Pamela's uncle had worked closely with the founders in their lifetime. It was no surprise, therefore, that Aunt Rosemary and her niece should have been invited to share viands with the senior members of the firm.

Pamela, in one of those sleek but unshiny dresses that she had convinced Aunt Rosemary were all the rage that year, gladly deferred to her aunt.

"I feel a hundred and eighty years old," Aunt Rosemary confided to Pamela. "And I felt so energetic this morning! But Sarah Purfrey just told me that she's to become a grandmother, which makes me feel even older."

Pamela looked over to Sarah Purfrey with a feeling of awe. The wife of Mr. Purfrey, though not as young as Pamela, had been considered a friend and an equal not too many years ago.

"Dear Lord!" she breathed.

"Your piety does you credit." Aunt Rosemary was amused. "There is nothing quite like marriage for separating women from their *femme sole* acquaintances."

Aunt and niece were the first pair into this banquet room. They were followed by Mr. Jonas Purfrey, who now held the bank's affairs in his hands. Mr. Purfrey and his family sat with them at the first table, which faced all the others. Supper was served in near-oriental surroundings. Looking down at the farthest table, where other guests were placed, Pamela saw a young man eating more lightly than anyone else. Half a dozen sips from the oyster soup were sufficient for him, with only a small portion of the frican-deau of veal, and he finished a charlotte russe and strong tea of a type with which Pamela had not previously been familiar. Long before their eyes met she had, of course, identified the tense young man as the Earl of Kinnon.

"What is *he* doing here?" she asked Aunt Rosemary, meanwhile thinking that the male of the species had been granted a distinct boon in the socially approved custom of even modified swearing.

"I was told by Sarah that Jonas has been of aid to the Earl in his hopes for a Cabinet position now or later," Aunt Rosemary replied. "I may tell you that business and politics are ever closely linked."

"The same concept has occurred to me," Pamela said wryly, earning a sharp look from her normally amiable relative.

Pamela stirred in the seat as a portly and red-faced Jonas Purfrey smiled at his much younger wife and stood to speak. Someone rapped a knife against the rim of the nearest crown goblet and called out, "The gaffer!"

"This dinner has been successful, as only eighteen dishes have been broken tonight," Mr. Purfrey began as Pamela tried to keep from meeting the Earl's sharp eyes once more. "And to those who may not have eaten to the full, there is a bin of apples by the door so you won't be hungry when you leave."

He paused for dutiful laughter. Swiftly engaging in the night's business, he presented twenty-pound bonus checks to the new "club members," as he called those who had served the bank for exactly twenty years. There was an added award to a somber, dapper clerk named Butterworth, a man who was of Welsh ancestry on his mother's side and whose pet project it had become to form a Forrest Bank choral society.

"And now I will keep you for only few minutes more," Mr. Purfrey said, signaling that it would soon be time for Pamela to address herself seriously to an avoidance of contact with the peer.

Mr. Purfrey spoke briefly about the death of Vincent Forrest and of how much the deceased gentleman's advice had meant. He added that Mr. Forrest's widow and niece, the last of the family which had founded the noble institution so dear to all their hearts, were among those present and that the bank owed a debt beyond repayment to the late Vincent Forrest's memory.

He sat down to sustained quiet that erupted in applause, starting from that end of the room where Kinnon was sitting, a tattoo of sound that grew louder as more and more joined in it. Women got to their feet with the men. Mr. Purfrey rose at the same time as Pamela.

Aunt Rosemary, flustered and misunderstanding the nature of the tribute, pushed back her own chair preparatory to rising.

It was Jonas Purfrey who reached over to put a hand on Aunt Rosemary's right arm and keep her in place.

"Stay," said Jonas Purfrey, making himself heard in spite of the roaring applause. "You, too, have been invaluable, my dear."

Pamela was already on her feet when the diners were eventually sent out to go their separate ways. Beyond the least doubt she wouldn't be able to avoid Kinnon, but she might make it clear past peradventure of a doubt that she wished any conversation between them to be perfunctory.

"I hope to speak with you," he said, so close that they almost touched. He wore a dark jacket over a bright waistcoat and white shirt with a collar tamped down over a bright-colored tie as if to keep it from jumping off. The lighting of this room was kind to his sunburned skin.

Because of close contact, Pamela found that her throat seemed constricted.

"I cannot feel that we have much to say to one another," she remarked, speaking as clearly as she could manage.

"But I rather disagree," he said with a judicious air that became him better than it became Avery Holt. "A considerable amount remains to be spoken, and in part that is because of information you may not yet have obtained."

She was keenly aware of the noises on all sides of her. Men and their families, on the way out of the banquet room, were discussing the evening that had just been concluded. A woman within Pamela's earshot rated the costumes of others of her sex. A man spoke about Mr. Purfrey's peroration and his general efficiency at work. Children were in a hurry to be gone. Occasionally two men could be observed in a colloquy.

Aunt Rosemary, herself deep in conversation with the Purfreys, must have noted from the corner of an eye that Pamela was speaking to the Earl. She held off coming closer as a result, presumably wanting to give the young spawn a chance to reach some understanding. In that hope, Pamela felt certain, she was misguided.

"I would think," said the Earl in the deep rich voice that she told herself had been thrilling in the past, "that you would be pleased about what has happened to Avery Holt and Miss Granbrook."

"What do you mean?" She experienced almost a stomach twist of pain at his assumption that she was gratified by her friend's fate. "What *could* you mean?"

"Why, they have gone off together, which I assume is what you wanted."

She hid astonishment at his colossal presumption but found it difficult to look directly at that handsome, strong-featured face and do so.

"Did this take place with your connivance?"

"Indeed it did." He smiled. "I made Avery the loan of my Rawlins carriage and my coachman as well. Since then, I may tell you, I have used the horse omnibus one time and when it started to rain I helped in urging the ladies to move downstairs while we gentlemen very properly replaced them in the open air. Such chivalry could lead to various indispositions over the next days, but those are well worth the risk if one can do the proper thing. Surely you concur."

The gray eyes probed at her, almost as if looking into her mind.

"It seems to me that I have not made my thought crystal clear," he said, "in the matter of Avery and Miss Granbrook. I have sent the two of them off to Gretna Green where they will be married quickly."

Pamela had, of course, heard and occasionally done some reading about that village in Dumfries in Scotland where runaway couples went to be married quickly with the help of a declaration before witnesses and the services of, she presumed, a dominie. That particular quirk in the Scottish law which allowed prompt weddings had been a source of amusement and wry speculation as well as offering a hint of romance existing somewhere in the British Empire. More than once even Pamela had imagined herself being carried away to Gretna Green, where the ceremony would be performed. Afterward, there would be an overnight stop at some roadside caravansary where the union would be consummated.

"You still aren't pleased." His lordship allowed a sigh to leave the confines of his lips. " 'Pon my word, you are a difficult woman from whom to elicit approval."

Pamela chose not to answer him directly. "Miss Granbrook's parents are unaware that it is marriage which is being contemplated."

"And that, too, is at my suggestion." The Earl seemed more pleased with himself than before. He was going to explicate the reasons for his cleverness. "If the parents had known in advance about the young couple's plans, they would have moved with might and main to reach Gretna Green quickly enough in hopes of keeping the marriage from offering them the chance to celebrate, if I might say so, what would be a *fête accompli.*"

Pamela's sensitive ears had weighed the pun and found it, along with the rest of Kinnon's explanation, sorely wanting.

"How could they possibly have arrived on time for that?"

"I don't know whether or not they could have, but one carriage breakdown and some other possible problems could have changed the course of this episode. 'All for the want of a horseshoe nail,' as some Yankee said about a battle that was lost."

Pamela shook her head fiercely. This was not the time to introduce such episodes as war and its casualties. Matters of greater immediate urgency impended here.

"And you are totally unaware of just what your meddling has accomplished?"

"My—did you say 'meddling'?"

"Certainly. As a direct result of your so-called

help and advice to the happy couple, Dilys' parents are so exercised that they will not forgive her."

"When she returns with a husband they'll change their tune."

"But the husband is not of the desirable sort that they had required," Pamela pointed out. "They will not forgive her for disregarding their instructions. Mr. Granbrook has made it clear that he will not agree to let Dilys into any home of his and Mrs. Granbrook's. The *fête accompli* of which you so frivolously spoke, your lordship, is more likely to resemble a *fête* worse than death."

"I still think that the Granbrooks will change their minds," his lordship averred stoutly. "Common sense impels a need for thought in alliance with the passage of time, Miss Forrest, and these have been known to work wonders."

She looked away briefly under the intensity of his gaze, as if he wanted to emphasize the words. Her anger deepened.

"Even if the Granbrooks do change their minds, it will not happen overnight, as you yourself have inferred. Years may pass before they utilize what you are pleased to call common sense."

He was moved now, his eyes narrowing in thought.

"That could be awkward."

"Most awkward."

"I will accept the emendation, Miss Forrest. Most awkward, yes."

"And it will be entirely due to your having interposed yourself."

"But I did that as a result of your suggestions to me," Kinnon remarked smoothly. "If there has been a difficult situation resulting, we are both to blame."

There was a disconcerting amount of truth in what he said.

Pamela acknowledged as much by her next words. "But what is to be done now?"

"I cannot say upon such a brief notification," Kinnon remarked. "However, should I be freshly inspired, you are the one with whom I will share my thought before putting any strategy into action."

"Yes, I would appreciate that."

They were smiling tentatively at each other before he took regretful leave to pursue a conversation with Mr. Purfrey.

It seemed to her upon only the briefest of reflection that the difficulty involving Dilys and

Avery had resulted in returning Kinnon to Pamela's good graces. Time would tell if his lordship could undo the damage he had done at Pamela's behest. Meanwhile she turned to Aunt Rosemary and engrossed herself in other matters.

CHAPTER 18

In Which It Is Shown That a Duty Can Be a Pleasure

Dilys had indeed trod upon the bridal path. Her marriage had taken place by means of a declaration before witnesses as made at the Gretna Hall, Avery having staunchly declined to let the ceremony be performed at the Sark Toll Bar or the smithy of more than local fame.

As man and wife, they crossed the Sark River bridge. At an inn in Cumberland he insisted on stopping, the decision made because Kinnon's coachman had informed him that the horses were weary. Mr. and Mrs. Holt would spend the night, Avery said magniloquently, in the finest style.

The innkeeper of the Goose and Gherkin, as this establishment was called, led them up in silence to a third-floor room.

"You can have hot water jugs right off, in case you be wantin' such," he offered then.

Avery turned down the offer. Dilys had a feeling that only with difficulty did he keep from smiling.

A bedstead had been jammed into the tiny room along with an octagonal table holding a gas lamp that lighted the wall motto—HOME IS WHERE THE HEART IS—done in red on a white background and framed under glass. Three wooden chairs had been placed at the foot of the bed. There was an inexpensive tile grate and enough space, it seemed to Dilys, for two thimbles but no yarn. As it happened, she soon realized that necessities could be accommodated in so small a space. It was a matter of definition.

The hot water containers, made of shiny stoneware, were brought after all. The dim-witted lad who fetched them was snickering as he closed the door.

Avery said quietly, "When you're ready, my dear, we'll go to bed."

She understood what he was really saying: he was willing to accept the thought that she must be so nervous as to delay what would soon be happening between them. Dilys shook her head, though. Hadn't both of them waited long enough already?

"When you turn away, I will disrobe," she suggested.

A mirror on the wall at her left showed Dilys her dark hair combed and parted fashionably in the middle. Her body was erect and trim. She had worn a day dress with much white in it, but some darker flecks as well.

The squeak of wooden chair legs across the wooden floor told her that Avery had pulled a chair over, and he was soon removing his own garb. It was placed neatly: collar and string-piece, waistcoat and jacket, trousers and shirt on the chair, hosiery tucked into the high dark leather boots.

And now she needed to do nothing else except disrobe in full, the dress first, petticoats afterward. The reflection of her unclothed figure showed a vulnerable but excited young woman.

Avery had climbed into the bed, considerately lying on his left side so as not to see her until she was ready. Dilys half hoped he would turn around for a long look at her flesh, then wondered why she should be prey to such undoubtedly wicked thoughts.

Avery shifted his body, presumably adjusting his height to the bed's size.

"Are you ready?" he asked.

"I don't think that Scottish solicitors are so impatient," she heard herself teasing him.

"I have never known a Writer to the Signet,"

he responded, and said nothing more on the subject. "However, I feel certain that their wives are dutiful."

No longer could her fate be put off, and she was anxious to learn more about one of the wifely duties of which she had heard in hushed tones for so many years.

Bending over to put out the lamp, she suddenly gasped.

"Hop into bed and you won't feel so cold," Avery said, misunderstanding the reason for this sudden change.

Quilt and sheet were raised as she climbed in, sheets icy to the body. Hot water containers hadn't helped any more noticeably than the balmy weather.

Avery stirred very slightly. She glanced at the back of his head and neck as well as at the top bone of his spine above the quilt and sheet. He was very young.

"Your mention of wives as a group has reminded me," Dilys began.

The timbre of her voice, distracted and upset, made him look around.

"What's wrong?"

"I was thinking of my elders."

Oddly enough, no consideration of them had

come to her since she had found Avery at his chambers and suggested that they run off together to Gretna Green. His feelings toward her, as she had known from the first, it seemed, paralleled hers toward him.

"And now," she concluded, "I don't know what is to be done."

"Nothing needs doing in that area," he said, perhaps a mite impatiently.

Bless him, he was the dearest man in the world, but without the slightest imagination!

"My pappa will be terribly upset and my mamma is certain to find it impossible to acknowledge that I am old enough to marry. She will feel the same way when I am fifty-five, perhaps, but at least she would have had time to accustom herself to the idea of a life for me away from her and Pappa."

"And you have not married the Duke of Wellington or some other wealthy peer," Avery remarked, bringing up an objection which Dilys had refrained from mentioning yet again as part of the catalogue of difficulties facing them. "However, a marriage has been performed, and we can enjoy the first pleasures of this union."

"Yes. Yes, of course."

"I realize that you are unsettled at the moment, but I see no need for that," Avery remarked as she might have expected. "You are not alone with the difficulty. Together, we will triumph over it."

She wanted to say that the triumph might take years and years to accomplish. Dickon Granbrook, despite all of the good points of his nature, was a notoriously stubborn man.

"I will try not to think of it now."

"Excellent, my dear." He may have been smiling. "In just a moment I am going to turn around. I won't pull the quilt off, or the sheet. Not on this occasion, at any rate."

Her expectation of difficulties, of troublesome and agonizing hours on this first night together, were not borne out. On the contrary, after the first moments, she found it a delicious and wonderful experience to learn a part of the meaning of that timeworn and previously exasperating phrase, "wifely duties."

At some time during the night Dilys awoke. After remembering nearly all of the recent experiences with the greatest of pleasure, she found herself once more considering her elders and their response to the recent ceremony and its aftermath. Avery would certainly help to smooth the troubled waters, but the experience was going to be galling and might require much patience and an expenditure of considerable time. It was a terrible way to begin her married life and his. No remedy suggested itself, however, none at all.

CHAPTER 19
A Stratagem Is Conceived

Ian Forrest, at the age of twelve, never hesitated about satisfying his curiosity. Rarely did it occur to him that he might be halted from doing so.

As a result, Ian didn't think twice about walking into his tutor's room late on the next morning. Mr. Gernald had been busying himself elsewhere about the Clifford Street house, as previously agreed upon between himself and Aunt Rosemary. Mr. Gernald's small and relatively airless quarters had a disconcerting freedom from what Aunt Rosemary called fripperies. Books were laid out on a small table and two hard chairs.

Ian, easily distracted, picked up a volume about United States Indians, with drawings of these persons dressed in loincloths and feathered headgear. Imagining himself as part of that very warm climate in the former colonies, as Mr. Gernald didactically referred to the United States of America, he could also imagine himself emerging from a long narrow structure as shown in one of the drawings, then taking a puff of the community pipe while in a rough circle with others, their sober faces raised to the bright sky. Wouldn't everybody he knew be envious!

His reverie didn't last long.

A gasp from nearby told him that Mr. Gernald was in the room and was furious. His tutor, affronted and astonished, faced him with fists on hips.

"You are in my room," Mr. Gernald remarked needlessly, his beard quivering as he pointed to the volume. "You are inspecting a book which I have not yet shown you because I have not yet torn out the indecent paintings."

"I didn't mean—"

"That is theft, in principle," Mr. Gernald snapped, reading the indictment with a mournful relish. "You seem entirely unaware of the difference between what is mine and what is yours, and this book is at the moment mine and no one else's."

Ian refrained from making the point that his Aunt Rosemary had undoubtedly paid for it.

As Mr. Gernald reached out both hands for the offending volume, Ian drew back reflexively. Mr. Gernald raised one palm that grazed the right side of Ian's jaw.

Too bemused to call out, Ian covered one cheek. The book was pulled from his hand. Mr. Gernald might even have aided this effort with a muffled oath.

Aunt Rosemary suddenly called out, "What has happened here?"

She stood in the doorway, glowering at both males.

The boy said quickly, automatically, "Nothing is wrong, Aunt."

Rosemary Forrest strode into the room and examined the line of Ian's jaw, touching it gingerly so that he protested at the added silky pressure. He had felt no hurt to speak of after Mr. Gernald struck him, nor had he wanted to risk any greater pain upon a subsequent occasion when an aunt might not be available to interfere on his behalf.

"I am well now," he said with almost perfect truth.

"You are a brave little man." Aunt Rosemary looked down fondly at him. "You must go to your room and rest, dear little one. If you need anything or feel ill, you may call one of the servants to notify me or your sister."

Ian nodded. He didn't often impose on the staff, though.

"No incident of this type will ever happen here again," she said, giving him one more tender look as he started to leave. By the time he was at the door those eyes had turned on Mr. Gernald. They were icy.

"I heard the blow, and I feel sure that you know what I expect you to do next," she said. "You shall receive your pay packet for the week, but you will be given only a qualified recommendation from me, and these are far more, in tandem, than you deserve."

An intense discussion of another sort entirely was proceeding in the downstairs sitting room. The double doors had been left open so that, even if this had been the time for such precipitate action, the Earl of Kinnon would have been indisposed to take Pamela in his arms and kiss her. As it was, he sat with hands on his lap and a concentrated, faraway look on those features which were handsome enough to convince Pamela for the dozenth time, at least, that he was undoubtedly much sought after by the ladies and other females.

"You have been deep in thought," said Miss Forrest at this point. "I have accomplished something."

His lordship didn't add that during the recent hours he had also been busily disporting himself in the House of Lords. He looked up, briefly defacing the right-hand pocket of his trousers. Any witnesses who called him distrait at this juncture would not have been misusing the Queen's English.

He proceeded to listen intently, however, as Pamela explained what she chose to call the new state of affairs. Early this morning, spurred by the dilemma, she had taken a carriage out to the home of her friend Miriam Packwood. Gaining admittance by subterfuge, she had explained to her friend what had happened, asking for assistance as well. She wanted Miriam and various other friends to take two-hour turns in mounting a watch on Bruton Street outside the Hotel Wimmer, sitting in carriages or walking the street if needs must. The one on watch when Avery and Dilys returned to her parents' temporary quarters would warn the young couple against the recently evolved attitude of Mr. and Mrs. Granbrook. A suggestion might be made that the newlyweds go elsewhere for a while. From another location Dilys could write to her parents and request an interview for herself and her husband, untitled though Avery might be.

"Aha!" said the Earl, having been apprised of this event. "At least you do not propose to beard the Granbrooks in their den."

Pamela had to nod. It was becoming apparent that not every conceivable crisis required direct action. To that extent, beyond peradventure of doubt, his lordship had intellectually impressed her.

In giving the brief summary, Pamela had excluded certain incidents. No mention had she made of the news that Miriam Packwood was on the point of becoming engaged to Viscount Brightwater, a fine young man with notably poor vision. Miriam was a splendid girl in character, as it happened, and would doubtless bear a plethora of children.

Nor did she mention the conversation with her onetime friend, Lady Suzanne Boyce. The daughter of the Marquis of Criddon, when run to earth after the greatest of difficulty, had indicated her keen regrets at being unable to help in what was doubtless a worthy cause. Her sympathies obviously halted at the lips. Pamela, who had hoped that the friendship might be reclaimed, was keenly aware that it was one of the casualties of the last chaotic weeks. She regretted the loss. Lady Suzanne was possessed of many fine if entirely superficial qualities. There were times when superficiality was desirable.

Kinnon, having blessed Pamela with his undivided attention, offered a thought on which none had to ponder.

"If there are enough friends to make up a satisfactory vigil, then it seems to me that something will indeed have been accomplished."

"Certainly."

"At least such a move might be helpful to Avery," his lordship pointed out. "Avery's career would suffer from a family scandal."

It was true but disconcerting to hear a male's interests being considered rather than those of a beleaguered bride.

"Should you be correct and the Granbrooks decline to see Avery and Mrs. Holt," Kinnon added pensively, "matters will be difficult indeed."

"Exactly. I have done what I could but that may not have been enough."

It was at this juncture that the sound of loud voices could be heard through the open doors. The voices hailed from an upper story. Pamela surged to her feet, prepared to investigate this outbreak of activity, but desisted at the sound of a woman's footsteps descending. A brief sojourn at one of the opened double doors was required before she pulled back as Aunt Rosemary rushed in. The two women were almost eye to eye.

"I have given Mr. Gernald his walking papers," Aunt Rosemary explained, adding details upon request. She had previously shown Kinnon the expected courtesies, so she contented herself now with a smile of recognition. "A new tutor must be engaged immediately."

"I can ask one of our multifarious footmen to convey your wish to the employment agency we use."

"Do so," the older woman agreed, then sighed and muttered, "And all because of a book with portraits of red Indians in loincloths."

The Earl courteously asked for further details. These were supplied. The word "loincloth" caused him to suddenly close his eyes and then open them wide. His lordship looked like one of those people Pamela had recently observed on Fleet Street walking from one bulletin board to another and down to the Ludgate Circus before entering the Devil Tavern, in most cases, with its hot mutton haunches that were supposed to be one of the tastiest repasts available in the purlieus of the City. By the time Pamela returned, her mission having been crowned with success, Kinnon had thrown his head back and was laughing.

"I appreciate humor as well as the next one, I should hope," Aunt Rosemary said, uncertain whether or not to be affronted. "However, it quite surpasses my doubtless feeble understanding to see the humor in this abysmal situation."

Kinnon collected himself as best he could. "I do beg your pardon. In this matter of Ian and his tutor, or of the Holts and Granbrooks, or of Miss Pamela and myself and our futures, there is, of course, nothing so base as humor, nothing whatever."

The very mention of humor caused him to resume laughing. Pamela, to be sure, found the merriment contagious and had to turn her back in hopes of not offending her aunt. Like the worthy Mrs. Forrest, she had no idea of the source of entertainment.

"I think I will leave the two of you to roll about in your hysteria," Aunt Rosemary said coolly. "At least you will not be perpetrating any baser social actions in the meantime."

With those sentiments, she took her departure.

Kinnon made herculean efforts to control himself, drawing deep breaths over and again.

Except for the barest beginnings of a twitch at the corners of his lips, he was successful.

"Please apologize to your good aunt in my name," he said finally. "I must tell you, if it is any justification, that the recent happening has permitted me to evolve the answer to our difficulty."

Pamela seemed dubious. "If you can reconcile Dilys with her parents and solely or largely do so because of paintings of red Indians in their loincloths—"

"Let us avoid that last word," Kinnon interposed swiftly. "After so many attempts at a solution, the word itself and the simplicity of the resolution which it connotes has a deleterious effect upon my risibilities."

"Very well, then. If you can accomplish the feat I have just outlined, or help Dilys and Avery accomplish it, I will feel that you have overruled all my previous objections to you as ever being thoughtless and unfeeling."

She didn't know why the gratuitous insult had been offered. Something in her made it necessary to say that if she eventually surrendered to him there would be a rational reason for the act.

"And if you are properly helpful," responded

the Earl of Kinnon with a genuine smile, "I will forget all of my previous objections to you as a bumptious and tactless young woman."

She crimsoned deeply at having been treated with the same delicacy that had distinguished her behavior toward him.

"What, then, is to be done?" she asked quickly.

Recalled again to the major matter of concern at this moment, Kinnon said, "When the happy couple appears in front of the Wimmer, I am to be notified."

"And what will you do then?"

Kinnon told her.

Pamela's eyes rounded in astonishment, then in full understanding. She did not laugh, although it was possible to sympathize with any temptation to make such a display.

"Do you think that the plan will prove effective?" For once she had asked a pointless question.

"We can but do the best that is in us," Kinnon answered with more tact than seemed called for, "and trust to the gods of confusion, indignation, anger, and resentment to bring about the desired resolution."

"In other words, you don't really know,"

Pamela said. "For Dilys' sake and for Avery's, I can but hope."

" 'And so say all of us,' " the Earl of Kinnon quoted somberly.

CHAPTER 20
Persuasion

The good fortune that occurred in the next hour was an augury, Pamela considered hopefully. Having informed Kinnon toward the end of their *pourparlers* that she was on her way to the hotel to watch for the appearance of the fugitive duo, Kinnon brightened up.

"By this time they are almost certainly on the way back to civilization," he said. "It occurs to me that if I may be permitted to accompany you on this jaunt matters could be expedited."

Briskly he led the way to the canoe landau, striding with such familiarity that an observer might have felt certain he was one of the family. Pamela, having taken moments to deploy a dark shawl and poke bonnet about her person at the proper places, followed with alacrity. Charity, the upper housemaid, had been conscripted to join them and make certain that Pamela's honor would not be violated. To this end, she had abandoned her Silver-O soap and Harkness brushes. Pamela wished that she herself was married if only so that her movements wouldn't require the companionship of an otherwise busy servant upon any occasion that might lure her away from the house in Clifford Street.

She glanced out at the sight of London in June, with Bennet Street sleepy in this early afternoon while St. James's bustled with activity. The coach moved lackadaisically toward Bruton Street.

Miss Miriam Packwood, who had been seated in her family vis-à-vis ten feet from the Wimmer, smiled, shook her head at Pamela to indicate that no newly wedded couple familiar to them both had arrived on the hotel premises, raised her brows in delighted surprise at sight of Kinnon, and drove off. A spinster aunt, who had accompanied her, looked as if she had been deprived of the elementary decencies of comfort.

Pamela and Kinnon sat in silence, her lips pursed while Kinnon's moved slightly but without speech resulting. There seemed nothing to say. Kinnon, like herself, was blessed with a strong practical streak, for which she felt duly grateful.

"Aha!" said the Earl suddenly.

Pamela's eyes followed his. Along the street

she could see a tangle between two carriages and what looked from here like a haywain.

"I couldn't mistake the mahogany on my Rawlins," the Earl added exultantly. And, as one carriage moved away and came closer, he said, "Nor could I mistake Scruggs."

Which, she recalled, was the name of Kinnon's coachman.

Apprehensively she followed his lordship out of the canoe landau. Kinnon walked spread-legged for once, like some sea captain on the deck of a new ship.

The coachman, discerning the presence of his employer, courteously pulled up before one of the iron hitching posts and awaited developments.

These were not long in transpiring. Kinnon hurried to one of the doors, opened it, and took two steps inside. With the coachman's discreet aid, Pamela soon joined him and the others.

By dint of some acrobatics she was able to embrace the new bride.

"You don't seem different," she said after the two had exchanged the warmest of greetings, "except, as far as I can see, for the eyes."

Dilys did not trust herself to speak of all that had taken place over the last days.

Kinnon, having extended felicitations to groom and bride, met Avery's shrewd eyes with his own and held them. His smile was warm and welcoming.

"You have brought back a treasure for yourself and I am happy on your behalf," he said, addressing Avery. "It is now necessary to keep that treasure superfine."

"I shall address myself to the task you indicate for as long as I live." Avery looked a little dazed, and Kinnon had noticed that his palms were as warm as coal in a scuttle.

"You will require, I fear, some aid in immediately doing so."

"I beg your pardon!" Avery began indignantly, but then swallowed. "You mean for establishing ourselves, of course. My family and my bride's will give such assistance as lies within their powers."

"Now there," said Kinnon, "speaks an optimist."

Dilys, more alert than her weakened groom, found her interest caught by the peer's speech inflection.

"I cannot testify about your father's reaction, which I think is likely to be suitable," Kinnon proceeded, "but there is information about the responses of the Granbrooks. It leaves, as the saying is, something to be desired."

"I shall win them over," the solicitor said, not visualizing even the slightest difficulty.

"Testing that out, my dear Avery, would be unwise at this time." Kinnon turned. "Miss Pamela, please inform our friends of what has passed between you and Mr. and Mrs. Dickon Granbrook."

Pamela did so in the fewest possible words, pausing only because Dilys called out and put up hands to her eyes. The gesture was merely *pro forma*, however, and Dilys was not in tears. It crossed Pamela's mind that if Dilys had married so quickly in part to escape the stringent supervision of her parents, it was a haste that could be justified at leisure. She was in control of herself and looked delighted to be inhabiting the same world as the tall solicitor. Avery, in his turn, seemed more than merely enamored. Together, they constituted a splendid argument for marriage if not for the necessity of having living relatives.

Avery relapsed into a silence inspired only in part by his pleasant weariness. By no means an imaginative young man, as has been pointed out, he was now able to foresee some difficulties in the necessary rapprochement with the esteemed parents of his bride.

It was Dilys, however, who conceived of a plan. "I shall go up by myself to speak with them."

"Do that," Pamela remarked, "and you will be shown the door."

Avery said stoutly, "I shall go with her."

"You," Kinnon said, "will not see the door as you will be ejected in the general direction of the Haymarket, with perhaps a slight spin as on a cricket ball that could take you as far away as Clapham."

Dilys, disregarding the scenic aspects of Kinnon's speech, had turned to her friend. "Do you tell me now that no direct action should be taken?"

It was a shrewd thrust. Pamela, great advocate of confronting difficulties as she was, found herself forced into taking the other side of the issue at this time.

"Not immediately, no."

The newlyweds looked at each other, silently considering the dimensions of the tangle that confronted them. Dilys nodded first. Avery, accepting that the fat was in the fire, turned to his friend and client.

"Have you any idea what is to be done?" he asked, as if a plan would be something of a supernatural manifestation.

"To quote you and Dilys as of a little while ago, 'I do.' " Kinnon said sunnily now. "Help is in sight if you agree to the course I suggest and refrain from burdening me with questions until time permits me to answer them."

Avery, of course, said promptly, "What sort of questions?"

Dilys gave an impatient exclamation, which she softened by a tender look. The shy young lady of only a few days ago, Pamela observed, was no longer so reticent in her private relations.

"You are to drive around the corner," Kinnon said, "and wait for my return in that." Almost casually, he pointed to the canoe landau, which stood nearby. It was the vehicle he would employ in the course of traveling.

Pamela stirred as he moved to the door, causing the Earl to look back.

"Please wait with the Holts," Kinnon said. "I cannot ask you to accompany me into the more questionable precincts of London."

Pamela nodded, if only at the thought of Charity's likely report to Aunt Rosemary if such an excursion was mounted at this time. Her own loyalty and high intelligence would currently be of scant use to Kinnon.

She watched him move out to the nearby carriage and instruct Charity to shift her custom over to the Rawlins, where her services as chaperone and general factotum wouldn't be of the least use either. Pamela sat back and waited for his return.

Dilys asked, "Are *you* able to answer questions? Surely you pried the truth out of his lordship."

One female was taking it as a matter of course that a female's wiles would be effective, which wasn't striking except that it was Dilys who spoke so casually on the subject.

"I will assuredly tell you what the Earl has in mind if you in turn make a promise, Dilys, not to do anything rash should you disagree with what is intended."

"The promise is made."

Reassured, Pamela let them know exactly what *modus operandi* the Earl was proposing. Dilys, her kind heart much in evidence, felt that draconian measures along those lines would be far too cruel for her dear parents. Pamela, who had considered the objection a while ago, pointedly disagreed.

Avery said mildly, "It is only offering them a display of what road your life could have taken had you not exercised your own judgment."

Dilys, about to dispute the point, looked at her young husband instead and her hand stole into his.

Pamela wished them well but sighed and looked out at the street in the direction from which the canoe landau would undoubtedly materialize in time.

The fight was under way in front of St. Olave's Grammar School on Tooley Street near the Tower Bridge Road. Two men were engaged, one with a knife that was at the moment rising in an arc. The other, far more confident, twisted the knife out of that dirty right hand, leaving the first to kick furiously.

Hampered by clothes, the more confident of the battlers was kept from hitting out effectively in the style of which he was normally an able practitioner. With one foot on the knife, thereby preventing its use as a weapon, the more confident one was taken wholly unaware when the losing contestant gave a surprisingly light shove before catching him with a wild punch on the temple and running off while the more confident combatant was recovering his balance.

The victor forced a smile for the benefit of the old man who'd been knocked to the gutter beforehand, causing the second man to interfere.

"Thank 'ee," the old man quavered. "Now I arter pay for the favor."

Disregarding the younger man's protest, he drew out a purse that was almost filled with enough coins to let the old man board for months, with hot meals included.

" 'Ere y'are, young fella-me-lad, with the 'earty thank 'ee of a poor but honest bloke."

And for perhaps saving his skin and certainly saving the moneys accumulated over a disreputable lifetime, the old man gave Ernest Osset a miserly threepenny bit.

Ernest, known to boxing aficionados as the Bermondsey Bleeder, as has previously been made manifest, looked bemusedly at the coin in his right hand while he wiped the freshly opened cut on his temple with the left. Engaged in these activities, he was unaware at first that a canoe landau was proceeding in his direction.

"Look for a fight near the leather goods area and you are certain to find Ernie," said the Earl of Kinnon cheerily from the depths of the carriage. "Our mutual friend, Terry, indicated to me that you would be close to the area at this time of day, and he was correct."

Ernest, who had understood three words out of every six, looked puzzled.

"What does yer want with me?"

"Thereby, Ernest, hangs a tale," said the Earl, adding a flourish to whatever riddle he might have been propounding. "Climb in while we drive to our destination."

Ernest glanced down at his clothes. "I ain't lookin' top 'ole, yer know, guv'nor."

"For my purpose, you will never look better," Kinnon said encouragingly. "Join me before the entire neighborhood hears how I am planning to enrich your coffers and then turns on you."

Ernest understood very few of those words either, but he raised a handkerchief to his temple to stanch the flow of claret and manfully ascended into the carriage.

CHAPTER 21
Pride and Prejudice

In choosing the Bermondsey Bleeder to carry forth that scheme which had been conceived as soon as the image of an unlettered personage in a loincloth was presented to him, Kinnon had made an unlikely but suitable choice. Ernest was fully capable of carrying out the effort which the Earl envisaged for him.

His willingness was spurred by the prospect of receiving some increment. Since winning a ring battle with unexpected speed as a result of Kinnon's bribe, Ernest had been unable to secure employment in the practice of fisticuffs. He had been reduced to occupying time by venturing upon pleasures oft experienced with various young ladies from Camberwell to Rotherhithe. His most successful tactic to this end, as he was a celebrity, consisted of informing the chosen female that he was unable to read and wanted an afternoon for lessons. Further, he was willing to pay for them. Arrived at his room, the girl was besieged by complaints that no one could make out those small squiggly shapes defacing white paper. She was soon besieged in different directions as well. Ernest may not have mastered the art of reading, but other skills were far from being beyond his capacities.

In a state of awe, he now listened to the Earl of Kinnon explaining the task that lay ahead.

"An' you want *me* for this lay, cully?" He was startled. "Not even to 'urt some bloke or other? Just to do what you say and nothin' more?"

"Certainly. We will be bringing two lovers together."

Ernest forbore to ask why the lover bloke couldn't bring his dolly to a rented room for the purpose. Members of a higher class, as he had been told, were different. Their idea of getting together involved churches, snarling parents who made the best of a bad job, and other needless features.

"Can I count on your help?" the Earl persisted. "Good man!"

The canoe landau halted near a more expensive carriage. The Earl emigrated and spoke to the people inside.

"All is well as of this moment," he said. "Now, Pamela, you are going into the lion's den."

"Very well," a young lady responded, her voice rising lightly. "We who are about to speak with the Granbrooks salute you."

Ernest would never in life understand how these people spoke to each other. He could hardly make out a word!

Mr. Granbrook, gloomy though he had been since his daughter's hasty departure from parental supervision, nevertheless rallied himself to discuss a household matter with his wife.

"Dorward came to me in the hallway," he said, referring to the butler who had accompanied them with other staff on their travels to Satan's duchy. "He has dismissed Mrs. Eviot, as of tonight."

Mrs. Granbrook's generous anger was instantaneous. "Why, she helped deliver Dilys and has been a mainstay of our family, as well as a splendid cook."

"I fear you will have to accept the inevitable, Olympia. Dorward claims that Mrs. Eviot has been insubordinate, disobeying a direct order."

"That's trumpery, Dickon, to force her out because she has been with us longer than anyone else and Dorward wants the staff to owe their fealty to him."

"Mrs. Eviot will come in to see me shortly, at my request," said Mr. Granbrook. The matter would not customarily have concerned him, but he had been responsible for the discharge of a maid not long ago and the memory rankled. Pamela Forrest, that disrespectful young woman, had crudely pointed out the unfairness of his actions. Rosemary Forrest, the widow of a friend and business associate, had indirectly bothered him by agreeing. His efforts in the current matter were an attempt to compensate for the previous wrong, if wrong it had truly been.

"I shall join the counsel between you and Mrs. Eviot," Olympia Granbrook said.

"No, you shall not." Her spouse was firm. "Dorward must be with the two of us, and I don't have the slightest wish to see you lose control of yourself."

"Then you must give Mrs. Eviot a chit!" The words were as close to command as Olympia Granbrook had ever come in dealing with her lord and master and shadow of God on earth. "That's the least we can do after all these years. If you refuse, Dickon, I shall see to it myself and even go against your wishes for once should they contradict mine."

"Mrs. Eviot shall have the highest possible references, I do assure you."

Mr. Granbrook paused at a mirror to make certain that his usual black suit and white shirt and string tie gave him the look of authority that would be required at the forthcoming Sanhedrin meeting.

"Even so, getting another situation will be very difficult for a woman of Mrs. Eviot's age," the mistress of the home declared.

"No doubt," Mr. Granbrook sighed. "Building a railroad is far easier than dealing with domestic problems."

With that apothegm spoken, he closed behind him the door to the small room he was utilizing as a study.

Waiting tensely, Olympia Granbrook could imagine what must have taken place. The lean-faced and competent Dorward would have walked into the truncated kitchen a while ago. Perhaps Mrs. Eviot had been resting in her armchair. At that point, Dorward would have snapped out that her employment was terminated without recourse.

Fists clenched, Olympia Granbrook felt almost as if she herself were being dismissed after long service. She could close her eyes and see herself addressing an imposing butler with respect, humbly asking for another consideration as befitted an inferior, pleading with eyes and hands, looking down at the aged body that had supplanted hers and was bereft of various aids to spurious youth.

Sympathetic consideration was more than she had usually offered to Dilys, her own daughter. But then, of course, the cook's advancing years were not a daily reproach to Olympia Granbrook, a daily reminder that she was herself aging rapidly.

Speculation about Dilys was of no use now and never would be again, it seemed. Dilys had been instructed to make a good marriage and had instead caught the contagion of disdain of elders, caught it from Miss Forrest, who was without true parents to instruct her. Dilys had run away with some Lothario! Never would Olympia Granbrook be permitted to hear the last of the episode after she returned to Castlerigg. Dickon had been largely restrained up to this point, but she rightly suspected that the major cause of such unexpected tolerance was the gloom into which he had been plunged by the press of events.

She heard a voice—perhaps Mrs. Eviot's—

raised in Dickon's study. Half running out of the sitting room, Olympia Granbrook strode to the door which Dickon had closed on her. She pulled back as it opened unexpectedly.

Mrs. Eviot, emerging, saw her and nodded, accepting the change in status. Olympia Granbrook felt as if she wanted to disappear in her best dress, to melt into the floor.

"Bless you," the cook said surprisingly, then took a step toward her and halted. Not long ago, Mrs. Eviot might have embraced her as a token of eternal friendship. Now, looking at the matron in her dark silk dress, Mrs. Eviot smiled weakly and then turned to hurry off. With a sinking heart, Olympia Granbrook knew that she would never see the good old woman again.

Dorward passed respectfully on his way out of the study before Olympia Granbrook tapped on the panel and walked in at her husband's growled consent.

"What happened?"

Mr. Granbrook's mind had again wandered to the agony posed by his daughter's betrayal. The question had to be repeated twice more, in an ever increasing loud voice, before he looked up.

"Mrs. Eviot has been placed on pension," he

said at last. "If she never finds another situation despite my reference, the pension continues until her death. Two shillings a week will not cause me financial distress at this time of life."

"Thank you," she said gratefully. Many another master would have chittered about hard times and let the cook go with her week's, but no more. "That is most generous."

"Mrs. Eviot is my first pensioner."

There was some minor commotion at the outer door. Olympia Granbrook went to see what was taking place, as it occurred to her that the cook and butler might again be despoiling each other's sensibilities.

In this instance, she was mistaken but shortly found herself wishing that she was not.

Miss Pamela Forrest had appeared at the door when it was opened by Dorward. Presumably the young woman's knock had previously been disturbing.

The hatchet-faced butler certainly recognized her and knew the extent of her disfavor with the family. The head of the house was not known as someone who generally kept his secrets. It would have been the work of a moment to close the door on her. Most likely, though, Dorward was offended that the cook had been sent away

The Reluctant Heiress

298

latter course would have been a demonstration
of what happened to any staff who gave Mr.
Dorward occasion to feel displeasure. As a result, he chose to take revenge by following the
letter of his duties.

"Yes, Miss Forrest?"

"I would like to see Mr. and Mrs. Granbrook," said the unbearable young creature. "It
is of the greatest importance."

"Please come in and wait, miss," the abominable Dorward said. "I shall inform Mr. Granbrook of your presence."

It would have been simple for Olympia Granbrook to call out that the butler should close the
door. On the other hand, his perfidy would be
made clear to Dickon when he entered the
study and transmitted the message. It is because
of such irritations that destinies can be altered,
as was shortly to appear.

Mr. Granbrook himself, having paused to
straighten some foolscap sheets on his desk, now
issued forth from the study in time to observe
what had taken place. He stood facing the
young woman in the poke bonnet and varicolored shawl, and her violet eyes met his.

Mr. Granbrook's anger at the butler caused

him, for once, to forgo the pleasure of losing his temper in the menial's presence.

"Come into the sitting room."

Pamela, unaware of the byplay and the reasons for it, was not surprised by the implied welcome she had received. It seemed natural to her that parents would want to learn as much as feasible about their daughter's present condition. Aunt Rosemary would certainly have responded similarly, if with greater courtesy.

Of these certainties she was soon disabused. The door closed on Pamela and both Granbrooks. Not even the autocrat of the home could have kept his wife from being witness to the happenings of the next moments.

Indeed, Mr. Granbrook's behavior soon recalled Pamela to sterner realities. A frown had settled in its accustomed lines about his features. He may have spoken more quietly than was his wont, but the tone vibrated with fury not unknown to those who dealt with him.

"We can have nothing whatever to say to you and nothing that you may communicate would be of the least interest to Mrs. Granbrook or myself."

Instead of being daunted by such palpable

hostility, the minx apparently felt herself challenged to proceed.

"Do you wish to see your daughter shortly?" Disconcerted though she had been, Pamela sounded confident that the answer would provoke a storm of maternal rectitude from Mrs. Granbrook and a few grunts from the father, the grunts to be followed by a nod.

None of these desirable happenings took place. Mrs. Granbrook waited indecisively beside the stuffed couch with its Chinese-pattern covering. Mr. Granbrook glowered down at Pamela, who had taken his favorite easy chair. Behind him was one of the numerous country paintings with which this apartment and so many rooms in London were cluttered, as if the residents worshiped outdoor life but wouldn't bestir themselves to take part in it. Of course that judgment was unfair in the case of the Granbrooks, who were, after all, visitors. But it seemed to Pamela, astonished by the silence, that few other adverse considerations about this couple would be hasty.

"I don't know any reason for seeing her," Mr. Granbrook snapped. "She has disregarded parental instructions about the future she should make for herself. Indeed, as you doubtless en-

couraged her to do, she has fled from the nur-
turing of her parents and adopted the company
of some London voluptuary."

Pamela brushed away all aspersions. "It will
interest you to know that your daughter is married. That much, I should think, is a source of
great comfort to you both."

Mrs. Granbrook gasped out, "My baby!" as if
Dilys had taken flight from the cradle and immediately crawled on all fours to the altar. "My
own baby!"

"Your daughter is no longer a baby." Pamela,
distracted, felt as if she had never heard such
nonsense in her life. "Dilys is old enough to
marry with a clergyman officiating at Gretna
Green."

Mrs. Granbrook snuffled. The point was one
that had inferentially been made by some of her
concerned friends at one time or another. Few
of those, and certainly not a wicked girl like
Pamela Forrest, would understand the tensions
that racked her life.

Mr. Granbrook, interrupting this conversation, which consisted of irrelevancies, said, "It
will interest *you* to know that I am planning to
leave this den of iniquity you call London and
do so in a day."

"Presumably you will be accompanied by your wife," Pamela snapped. She had come on a peacemaking mission but it seemed impossible for her not to be affronted by this pair. In another mood she would have admitted to the strengths of their characters, but this wasn't the mood.

Mr. Granbrook eventually nodded to indicate that his wife would accompany him back to the safety and undoubted probity of Castlerigg and its residents.

"As Dilys is married to a commoner," Mr. Granbrook continued, "she has been disobedient to her parents. For that reason, in spite her respectability, we have no wish to see her."

It was on the tip of Pamela's tongue to say that the constricting attitudes of both elders had driven Dilys to a hasty marriage, although it might prove a happy one after all.

Nonetheless, she had to keep in mind the commission that had brought her to this lair for a very special occasion. Much against her personal inclinations, it was necessary, at Kinnon's insistence, to deviate sharply from actuality.

"Anyone who tells you that Dilys is wed to a commoner is tampering with the truth," she said in what she hoped was a sufficiently sharp tone.

The Granbrooks exchanged glances, and the female half of the duo touched a knuckle to an eye and looked mournful.

Pamela, teeth gritted, waited for her to say, "My baby!" once more, and was unsurprised, as a result, when those inflammatory words were spoken.

"Dilys is *not,*" she began, and then tried to clamp her lips shut. Dilys Granbrook's age and sentient state were not the overriding issues at this meeting.

Dickon Granbrook was swaying back and forth, hands immured in his pockets. It was his interest and approval that had to be won immediately, as Pamela was well aware. At this time the railroad builder was in two minds about whether or not to express them.

Nonetheless, in his thoughts he must be accepting the possibility that Dilys, by marrying someone with a title, had followed the orders of her family. Some interest could be expressed as a result.

"She married a Knight Bachelor, I suppose," the bride's father suggested, demonstrating a vein of humor that few of his acquaintances suspected. "That would be appropriate."

Pamela breathed a sigh of relief. The Rubicon had been crossed. It was more like the Styx, on second thought, with one of the passengers doing further duty as Cerberus.

"Possibly he is a Companion of Little Honor," Mr. Granbrook continued, unwilling to abandon this jocular vein of speculation. "I have just thought of that title."

"Your daughter is the wife of a Noble," Pamela insisted. It seemed impossible for her to speak the exact lie that she had been primarily sent here to enunciate. Not even her antagonism to the behavior of these people could easily persuade her into it.

"My baby!" Mrs. Granbrook's eyes widened and her conception immediately embraced the lowest of peerage titles. "A—a Baron?"

"My daughter would not settle for a Baron," Mr. Granbrook responded crisply, his posture a little more rigid. He had stopped swaying on the balls of his feet. "A Viscount, at the very least."

"You are both too modest in your aspirations for your daughter and my friend." The lie must be spoken now, and in an even tone of voice. "Dilys has become the wife of an Earl."

"An Earl!" Mrs. Granbrook put a knuckle to her heart, as if the organ would be kept placid by such a measure. "He—he sits in the Lords, then."

"Certainly," Mr. Granbrook said with a fine air of disdain. "My eldest grandson will be a Right Honorable from birth, and the younger sons will be Honorables."

Mrs. Granbrook nodded in awe. To neither parent had it occurred that their daughter might give birth to one or more females. It was a supposition that Pamela would have vigorously disputed on any other occasion.

Caution had been repeatedly urged by Kinnon while giving instructions. The Granbrooks must not be antagonized one jot or one tittle more than necessary.

"My grandsons will all of them attend Balliol," Mr. Granbrook said, allowing no opposition. "It had always been my ambition to attend Balliol or have a son there, but grandsons in attendance will have to suffice."

"My father attended Keble, you know," Mrs. Granbrook offered hesitantly.

"Yes, for only three days." Mr. Granbrook dismissed his late father-in-law's scholastic at-

tainment, such as it may have been. "My grandsons will attend Balliol."

Pamela wished she didn't suddenly feel sorry
for the Granbrooks, as they were about to live
through a difficult time. She hoped it wouldn't
be of too great a duration, but there seemed no
way of avoiding it and also insuring the eventual
happiness of Dilys with Avery.

"Your daughter, as you now know, has been
good and dutiful. She has been faithful to the
precepts with which she was inculcated. She did
run away, but only to marry more quickly and
embark with greater celerity upon relations with
her husband." It occurred to Pamela that she
was making these points clear to the meanest
intelligence.

Mr. Granbrook's complexion turned a curious
color which had almost certainly not appeared
in those precincts until that moment. He swallowed and nodded, then, and the color of his
skin returned to its apoplectic normality.

His wife, who had never taken enjoyment
from what were called relations, simply nodded
and kept feelings of puzzlement to herself. A
question, however, did occur to her.

"Where did she meet him?"

Unprepared for this diversion as well as any of

the others that had materialized in the last minutes, Pamela was nonetheless unable to avoid a response.

"At a boxing match," she blurted out, giving voice to those words that first occurred to her.

Mr. Granbrook was startled. "My daughter would not attend such a contest."

"Her husband-to-be, as he was at that time, was one of the contestants. His sobriquet in the ring is The Boxing Peer."

"Certainly it is an avocation," Mr. Granbrook said with difficulty, although he appeared to have swallowed something sour to the taste. "It ought to be pointed out that he could be seriously damaged in the course of such a contest."

Pamela felt that any further pursuit of this matter while she was alone with the Granbrooks would cause her to scream.

"Then I can assume that you would like to meet the Earl and his Lady."

"Very much so."

"They are now awaiting your collective pleasure."

"Both are in the hotel? Dilys and his lordship should certainly be admitted here, and as soon as may be."

To this schedule, Mrs. Granbrook entered what Avery would have called a demurrer.

"In ten minutes," she said with a disapproving look around her at the room that seemed spotless to everyone else. "Let the staff clean up as much as they can in that time."

"I see no disarray," Mr. Granbrook protested.

But his capacity to dominate Olympia Granbrook was not proof against her wish to make the suite impeccable to a peer's eye.

"I don't want an Earl to think that we are untidy," she said strongly.

Mr. Granbrook offered no further opposition.

"In ten minutes, then," he said as Pamela rose. "Not one moment longer. I will not have my daughter and son-in-law kept waiting unreasonably."

More than twelve minutes passed before there was a knock at the door of the Granbrook suite. Dickon Granbrook himself, not wanting the impossible Dorward to be in sight until his animosity toward the butler was minimized, opened the door.

The sight that confronted him was memorable by any standard. Dilys stood ill at ease with her hand on the arm of a chunky man who was bleeding lightly from a cut on the temple.

Pamela, at the right of the pair and just out of Mr. Granbrook's sight, spoke triumphantly.

"This gentleman is the Earl of Kinnon," she said.

At which point, offering a smile that betrayed an almost complete absence of teeth in his head, Ernest Osset, the Bermondsey Bleeder, stepped forward.

CHAPTER 22
Sense and Sensibility

Volumes have been composed by other distinguished scriveners with the intention of plumbing the depths of anguish in certain human beings. The present chronicler, daunted by the task, draws the curtain of belated decency over the next moments.

Let it suffice to say that Mr. Dickon Granbrook's features grew red and that his wife's jaw dropped unbecomingly. With that, perhaps, the more charitable reader will be content.

" 'Appy ter know yer, guv," said Mr. Osset, having enfolded Dickon Granbrook's hand in his. Although he put on the very lightest of pressures, the gesture sufficed to cause Dickon Granbrook to wince.

But that worthy made no comment until after Mr. Osset had kissed Olympia Granbrook on a cheek and called her "the best mum any girl ever 'ad, I bet."

Mr. Granbrook said, "I do not believe what is happening before me."

A droplet of blood from Bermondsey's temple had drifted onto Mrs. Granbrook's chin. Forsaking an invaluable knuckle, she wiped at it furiously with a square of cambric.

Mr. Granbrook, staring at his daughter, said, "This—*this* is your husband?"

Pamela spoke quickly before Dilys could throw herself on the mercy of the court and confess all. "The Earl is considered an ornament to the peerage, and rightly so."

Mrs. Granbrook, for once as weak and dizzy as she looked, said, "And you met at a pugilistic contest?"

Mr. Granbrook suggested, "No doubt the Earl was bleeding, and drops fell into our daughter's clothing." Adversity was causing him to become a humorist.

"Dilly is a wonderful girl," Bermondsey asserted fondly in his role as the Earl of Kinnon. They had been introduced awkwardly only moments ago.

" 'Dilly.' " The pain was almost too exquisite for Dickon Granbrook to bear. "I would like to hear the happy bride tell me that this man is her husband."

Dilys promptly burst into tears. Confronting him, more than her mother, offered difficulties

which the young matron had not wholly anticipated.

Pamela said, "She is crying tears of happiness."

Ernest Osset, carried away by his role of peer,
leaned forward and bussed Dilys soundly on a
cheek. If anything could have caused Dilys
Granbrook Holt to leap like a scalded cat, this
would have been the stimulus for such behavior.
At the moment, however, she was far too
stunned by the proceeding of which she was a
part.

Mr. Granbrook indicated that he was beyond
speech, a condition unlikely to prevail.

Ernest, made more awkward by the pro-
tracted silence and aware that the discussion
had briefly touched upon the manly art of deci-
mating an opponent, smiled almost toothlessly
once again and showed his fists.

"Best pair o' fives in Bulldom, if I does say so
meself," Ernest insisted. "Next time I gets
Knightsbridge in me lamps, I'll make mince pie
o' him, you see if I don't!"

Pamela put in smoothly, "Boxing is the Earl's
favorite sport."

"An' I want yer all to be there," Ernest went
on, further stirred by the contact with a higher

class of person than he normally encountered. "Mum, Dad—if I might call yer that, guv, seein' as 'ow we are all family now."

Mr. Granbrook was moved to permit an exclamation very much like a hiss to escape between the confines of his lips.

Dilys, having heard this sound of muffled agony for the first time from so august a source, suddenly called out. Every eye, as could be expected, turned toward her.

"I—I can't go on with this."

Pamela, knowing the girl as well as she did, realized that the truth had been spoken. Dilys was close to the end of her tether.

It was Mr. Granbrook whose attitude was the surprise to Pamela at this time. He looked away from Ernest as if the Bermondsey Bleeder wasn't in the room.

"This has been arranged as a cautionary episode, has it not?" he asked softly.

"Y-yes, Father."

Pamela felt as if she wanted to turn and run off. For the first time she wondered that she had found the real Kinnon persuasive enough to enlist her services in this *folie à trois*, as she now thought of it.

Dickon Granbrook probed further. "Your

friend felt that the family insistence upon you marrying a peer above all other specimens of humanity was deserving of a warning about such narrow vision. Am I correct?"

Dilys nodded.

Mrs. Granbrook had listened unbelievingly as her husband spoke and watched in a similar state when her daughter moved her head.

"Then you are not married," said the matron, and it grieves an assiduous chronicler to report that there was a note of hopefulness in the mother's voice.

Dilys shook her head.

"You *are* married." It was Mr. Granbrook who correctly interpreted this gesture of his daughter's. "Because of our hectoring you went out and married the first man who attracted you and to whom you were attracted."

Dilys looked away. "I do love him," she whispered.

"It behooves your mother and myself to be of all possible assistance, then," said Mr. Granbrook. "I assume that he is a commoner."

"Yes. He is a solicitor."

"Then at least he will not be reduced to rifling the contents of poor boxes in church," Mr. Granbrook said, with a touch of his customary imperiousness. "There is much to cause calmness in that news."

For the first time Dilys met his eyes but did not bring herself to speak.

"And I take it that he awaits the results of this chicane." He glanced narrow-eyed at Pamela.

The implied accusation was too much for Pamela's hard-won restraint. Unable to deny that she had participated in the hoax, she briefly ignored her feelings of regret to make a strong riposte.

"No matter how you may feel about it at this time, I can assure you that your daughter has married a good and honorable young man and one of whom you need never be ashamed."

Granbrook fell silent, his lips drawn tightly together. Mrs. Granbrook searched out part of the cambric square that wasn't bloodied and wiped her cheeks.

Ernest Osset looked confused, his mouth wide open, eyes in motion from left to right. It was as if the Knightsbridge Knave or one of his other rivals in the art and craft of fisticuffs had got beneath his guard and stunned him.

Pamela said, "It is time for us to be leaving, Bermondsey."

"Yerss!" At the door, the pugilist turned to look back. "I 'opes yer don't 'old this little game against me. I was put up to it, I was!"

His audience was entirely unresponsive.

"Yer all still welcome to see me squash ol' Knightsbridge to a pulp," he added, offering the greatest inducement to forgiveness that was in his power. "Bleed like a pig, 'e will! You think you've seen some bleedin', when I get done with 'im you'll know what bleedin' really *is!*"

Pamela found it a more arduous task than she might have expected to persuade Ernest to leave, and finally had to use a peremptory tone of voice to accomplish that desirable objective.

CHAPTER 23
"All Are Safely Gathered In. . . ."

Pamela returned home in the canoe landau, grateful that the ghastly business was over. She had sent Avery up to the second floor of the Wimmer to join his bride and in-laws. It was hoped that the recent sight of Bermondsey as a family member would cause the Granbrooks to welcome Avery with open arms, or at least a cautious reserve instead of icy hostility. Neither Kinnon nor his invaluable brougham was anywhere in sight.

. She found only the most minor of difficulties back at Clifford Street. Ian and Aunt Rosemary were at odds over the appointment of a new tutor. Pamela sensibly cast her vote on Ian's side, remarking that the boy would have to learn from some man he could respect and admire. Aunt Rosemary had to agree eventually.

Alone in her room at long last, Pamela dressed for supper. Careful thought caused her to choose the lilac with its lace-edged front, a combination which accented the fiery red of her hair if it did little for the violet eyes. Best of all, the roundness of her face, which she always imagined would put off anyone but a painter of Dutch burghers like the late Mr. Breughel, was diminished. An examination in the square mirror that she favored for such inspections was enough to confirm that impression for perhaps the hundredth time. She regretted having to wear the narrow-tipped shoes with heels almost high enough to please Dilys when in the company of her husband, but none others were available to give her feet that click-click of authority when she moved.

She was occupied by these reflections when Aunt Rosemary appeared at the door.

"Your effort has not been in vain," said she, casting a look of approval at the rig-out. "He is here."

" 'He'?" Pamela gathered her faculties. "Do you refer thus to the Earl of Kinnon, the Queen's Right Trusty and Right Well-Beloved Cousin, as he and other Earls are officially known?"

"Of course I do."

"Send him away," Pamela said decisively, perhaps taken aback by her aunt's momentary irritation. "Perhaps the Queen will offer comforting words to him."

"Didn't you expect a visit from Kinnon?" Another look at the rig-out. "You have dressed quite to the crack, as it used be known in my youth, for supper *en famille*."

"I have no wish to see or speak with Lloy—his lordship."

"You should certainly have expected him after this day's previous doings," Aunt Rosemary said, a bit pettishly. Pamela had, of course, made a confidant of her in the matter of purifying the Granbrooks with terror, if not pity. "You could previously have written the Earl to say that you will not be at home to him. If, that is, you truly have no wish for his presence."

"You are implying that I crave to see him, but in truth I do not."

"In that case, I will inform the Earl of your antipathy and ask him to leave."

"Do so," Pamela said, hesitating only because she wanted to make another turn to the left and inspect herself in the glass from the angle that was accordingly presented. No other reason would have caused her to delay responding, of course.

"Very well, then." Aunt Rosemary paused,

considering. "I have first to speak with Charity about a minor kerfuffle so that a few minutes will pass before I am able to convey your message to his lordship."

Her aunt was under the impression that Pamela's mind would be altered after briefly considering the position of matters. Pamela, with no intention of doing so, let alone of seeing a man toward whom her anger had become all-consuming, decided that she would tell him the truth herself in the fewest but most pointed possible words. It would put finis to the entire misbegotten courtship imposed on both of them from without, a courtship that could offer no happiness to either if it was resolved in marriage.

Lifting the dress to keep her from taking a possible header, Pamela walked quietly to the carpeted stairs and made her descent. The forthcoming interview would take only moments and she would then be able to enjoy a hearty supper in the bosom of her dear family.

The Earl of Kinnon had almost certainly been pacing the large sitting room until such patience as he possessed was worn down. He had emerged into the hall and was looking bemusedly at a dark statue of an oriental personage. At the sound of Pamela's heels striking the floor he turned.

The light gray eyes rested upon her, pleasure dampened by observing the set of her lips and narrowness of her eyes.

"So you are still here," she began flatly.

"I have in my time been made welcome in a far more florid fashion," the Earl said, and was alone in smiling at the remark. "Might I ask what heinous crime I have now committed to irritate you so?"

Pamela was silent, unable to marshal words for what Avery Holt would have called the indictment.

"I think that I am entitled to that information, if only on the grounds of courtesy such as one might display to a complete stranger."

She was, of course, stung. "How can you ask such a question!"

"By maneuvering my tongue and lips, if you don't really know—just a moment! I gather that something of moment has come up to exercise you, but I have no way of telling what it might be. I am aware only that you felt strongly I must manage a rapprochement between Avery's wife and her parents so that they would approve of him. By doing so I could be deemed worthy of your hand in marriage. Am I misstating any of the facts?"

Pamela sniffed, which was an admission of sorts.

"It will perhaps be of interest to you that I have spoken with Avery since that meeting. He has gratefully told me that Mr. Granbrook has become an admirer of his, an attitude spurred by Avery's instructing his father-in-law about the legal steps needed to convert his home into a limited liability company with a registered share capital of one hundred thousand pounds, most of it to go into Mr. Granbrook's capacious pockets, I assume."

Pamela found an objection. "I hardly know what those words mean."

"I share your innocence up to a point, but I gather that the land connected to Mr. Granbrook's home is productive, and the explanation may be illuminated by that knowledge." Kinnon's smile was a pointed reminder yet again of how truly handsome he was. "I ask you to remember that Avery and Dilys and her parents are now friends, and this has occurred solely because of my plan and its spirited execution."

"Your scheme, as I feared but later overlooked, was cruel and heartless," Pamela said now, inflamed by what she considered was his smugness. "I am ashamed that I should ever have been part of it by deceiving the Granbrooks."

A light dawned behind Kinnon's gray eyes. "So that's it! You are stirred because the Granbrooks were initially upset."

"And that I was responsible for it in part," Pamela snapped. "And that I let you persuade me into participating in the cruelty."

"You are saying that my suggestion was a cruel one," the Earl summarized. "Permit me to make one inquiry: was Mr. Granbrook deceived by seeing and hearing someone like Ernie Osset claim he was an Earl of the Empire? Was he deceived for so much as a moment?"

Pamela retreated strategically from this outpost of debate. "Even if it were true that he wasn't deceived, would it be a justification of your cruelty?"

"What would have taken place otherwise?" the fourth Earl of Kinnon asked reasonably enough.

Pamela, who had been silent from anger only a few minutes ago, was reduced to an inability to answer that was caused by embarrassment.

"Avery would have had no chance to gain his

father-in-law's esteem, thereby causing his wife great unhappiness. Dilys would have been estranged from those blood relatives who raised her. As for the Granbrooks, for whose feelings you have constituted yourself so persuasive an advocate, they would have been in the depths of misery because of what they thought had taken place."

Pamela had to concede in part. "The Granbrooks may be difficult, but they are not wicked." It was a point she would not have considered in the past when all who thwarted her had to be perceived as monsters of wickedness. "They have sorrows of their own, I feel certain, which cause them to say what they sometimes do."

"As which among us does not," Kinnon agreed, having adopted a policy of verbally underlining the obvious in order to win this crucial argument. "Nonetheless, it is apparent to me that you can be moved to compassion even for those with whom you may differ. I ask you to extend this range of emotions to my own self."

Amused in spite of herself by this fresh conceit, Pamela was on the point of grinning.

"After all that has happened," she asked slowly, "would you still want to plight your troth with somebody as difficult to win as I have proved myself?"

"You have proved yourself to be the girl who has a breadth of sympathy and a willingness to listen and consider the views of others."

One more objection had to be interposed. "There are people who will accept it that the marriage would have been agreed upon by both of us, but others might feel that you would be marrying for my dowry."

"Hang your infernal dowry!" Kinnon snapped. "Give it to some charity."

Pamela did grin now. "My Aunt Rosemary will be able to commence a new charity with my assistance, as I suggested to her not long back."

"That should give an added rein to your inclination toward helping others—forcefully if necessary."

A riposte was demanded to this sardonic comment. "But what will put a halter on your inclination to be mistakenly secretive and devious and roundabout?"

"Why, you will." Kinnon looked surprised that the question should be raised. "For example, you have been causing me to declare myself to a greater and greater extent from the second time we met. (I would have loved you on the first occasion, but I had no prolonged chance to speak with you during our brief gyrations about the dance floor at that time.)"

"I am flattered, but I see no sign that my humble efforts are succeeding," Pamela said, pointedly raising her face to him.

He grinned and advanced, fully understanding what was wanted.

"Perhaps you will accept proof of my assertion," he said.

Aunt Rosemary, descending the stairs at that moment, was the witness to the next development. His lordship embraced Pamela and his lips were lowered to hers. Pamela's arms hurriedly went around Kinnon's shoulders, to the watcher's delight as well as his lordship's, and the pressure of Kinnon's lips was joyously returned.

It was a chuckling Aunt Rosemary who made her way softly to the rear of the house and a brief discussion with the downstairs maid.

"Please set another place for supper, Hope," she said. "The delay should offer sufficient time for two young persons to compose themselves, but I am happy to say that I cannot be absolutely certain of it."